Books by Paula Williams
in the Linford Romance Library:

PLACE OF HEALING

FINDING ANNABEL

Annabel had disappeared after going to meet the woman who, she'd just discovered, was her natural mother . . . However, when her sister Jo travels to Somerset to try and find her, she must follow a trail of lies and deceit. The events of the past and the present have become dangerously entangled. And she discovers, to her cost, that for some people in the tiny village of Neston Parva, old loyalties remain fierce and strangers are not welcome . . .

PAULA WILLIAMS

FINDING ANNABEL

Complete and Unabridged

LINFORD
Leicester

First published in Great Britain in 2011

First Linford Edition
published 2012

British Library CIP Data

Williams, Paula.
  Finding Annabel.- -(Linford romance library)
  1. Love stories.
  2. Large type books.
  I. Title II. Series
  823.9′2–dc23

ISBN 978–1–4448–0995–4

Published by
F. A. Thorpe (Publishing)
Anstey, Leicestershire

Set by Words & Graphics Ltd.
Anstey, Leicestershire
Printed and bound in Great Britain by
T. J. International Ltd., Padstow, Cornwall

This book is printed on acid-free paper

1

Graham Frankley had not been expecting to die that foggy February morning. Had he done so, being the caring father he was, he'd have put his affairs in order and not left his two grieving daughters the agonising task of clearing away the remnants of his last hurried breakfast or all the other heartbreaking detritus of a life cruelly cut short by a jack-knifing tanker on a greasy motorway.

He'd have also kept his promise to his wife who'd died of cancer fifteen long, lonely years earlier.

'Promise me you'll tell Annabel the truth,' she'd begged. 'We should have told her years ago and I'm sorry I stopped you. Only don't tell her yet. I know I'm being a coward but I simply can't face it. Not now. Besides, she's having enough trouble at the moment dealing with my wretched illness. But

1

later. Promise me you'll tell her later when the time's right.'

So he'd promised. He'd tried several times to keep that promise and on the evening of her eighteenth birthday he almost succeeded. But as he struggled for words, the moment passed and he missed his chance. Each time he put it off, the harder it became.

Until that last February morning. Now there was no more time. No more chances left.

So it had lain there, at the bottom of the rosewood writing box, a small, carefully-folded piece of paper, tucked in between the girls' baptism cards. Waiting to be found and dealt with, like the phone bill, the car insurance and all the other bits of unfinished business.

★ ★ ★

'Thank goodness you're there, Jo. You were such an age answering the phone, I began to think you'd taken the afternoon off.'

'Annabel?' Jo sat up straight in her chair, alerted by something in her sister's voice. 'Are you all right?'

Annabel gave a short laugh. 'Yes, couldn't be better.'

'You sound a bit — a bit odd. Is something wrong?'

'Nothing's wrong. Quite the reverse, in fact. I've found her, Jo. I've found my mother. After all these months, I've finally tracked her down. I haven't met her yet, only spoken to her on the phone, but she sounded okay. Really nice, in fact.' Annabel gave another short laugh, high pitched and breathless, the way she always did when she was trying to cover up the fact she was nervous. 'She said she was looking forward to meeting me. It's really happening, Jo. I still can't believe it but I'm actually going to meet my real mother.'

Jo let the pen she'd been twisting between her fingers clatter to the floor. 'In case you've forgotten, our mother died fifteen years ago,' she said in a cold, tight voice.

'Your mother,' Annabel snapped back sharply. 'Your mother died back then. Not mine.'

Jo prayed for patience as she bent to retrieve her pen. 'How can you say that? Mum and Dad were as much your parents as mine. They loved us and treated us equally — you know they did.'

'Equally? Easy for you to say. You weren't the one who'd been lied to all your life. To me, finding my real mother — '

'Your birth mother,' interrupted Jo.

'Okay. Okay.' Annabel's voice crackled with impatience. 'Finding my birth mother is as much about finding myself as her. I need to know who I am, where I came from and why she gave me away. You can't possibly imagine what not knowing feels like.'

'Look, I do understand, Bel, honest I do,' Jo said soothingly. 'And you know I'd do anything to help you through this.'

Her heart ached with pity as she recalled the cruel way Annabel had found out she was adopted. It had been almost a year ago now, a couple of days after their father's funeral and they'd been going through the grim task of sorting through his things.

Even just thinking of that time evoked the musky fragrance of the old rosewood box that held the documents that charted their parents' lives: medical cards, passports, births, marriage and now death certificates. And the feeling of shocked disbelief that still clung to herself and her sister.

Then, at the bottom, tucked between two faded baptism cards was the piece of paper that had turned Annabel's world upside down. Her Certificate of Adoption.

'Don't think I'm not grateful for all your help,' Annabel's voice was softer, more conciliatory now. 'Goodness knows, I couldn't have got through the last year without you which is why I'm phoning now. You've been with me all the way so far and I'd really like it if you would come with me.'

'Come where?'

'To meet her. I'd really like it if you were there.'

Annabel had talked of little else but tracing her birth mother since finding the papers and Jo was glad for her sake that her search was over at last.

'Of course I will. It's not something you should do on your own.' Jo reached in her bag for her diary. 'When are you meeting her?'

'I'm not sure. Sometime today or maybe tomorrow.'

'So soon? But can't it wait until — ?'

'I can't wait,' Annabel said firmly. 'She's going to get back to me about where and when. I've tracked her down to a little village and I had to promise I wouldn't tell a soul. So you've got to promise as well.'

Jo glanced at her watch, horrified to see it was 2.15 already. Where had the day gone? 'I promise. But, look, I really must — '

'It's called Neston Parva which is on the Somerset Levels, the middle of nowhere by the sound of it. You've got to come with me, Jo. You're the only one who can stop me opening my mouth and putting my foot in it.'

'Of course I will, but — '

'You know what I'm like when I'm nervous. I say the first thing that comes into my head. And I'd hate to come out with something like 'Good to meet you. Now I can see who I get my hideous nose from,' and mess things up before we've had a chance to say hello.'

'But you don't mean today, surely?' Jo finally managed to say as Annabel paused to draw breath. 'I'm still at work. Even if I left now, which I can't because I'm absolutely snowed under, it would take at least three hours to get down to Somerset.'

'That's all right. Come down this evening and I'll say we'll meet her tomorrow. I'm staying in this really great hotel in Wells. That's where I'm calling from now as a matter of fact.

You'll love it. Blazing log fires, oak-beamed ceilings. Dripping in history. It's definitely your sort of place, Jo.'

'But I can't,' Jo said, dismayed. Of all the weekends, why did it have to be this one? 'I've made plans to go away.'

'In the middle of January? Where?'

Jo glanced around the office. Even though no one was looking in her direction, she lowered her voice. 'I'm going to the New Forest with Matt,' she said. 'He's got a cottage there.'

'I'll bet he has,' Annabel gave a harsh laugh. 'Honestly, I don't know what you see in him.'

Annabel and Matt had met briefly over Christmas and to say they hadn't hit it off would be an understatement. She thought he was arrogant and manipulative, while he'd made no secret of the fact he thought Annabel was spoilt — and manipulative. *Maybe*, Jo thought with a wry smile, it took one to know one.

'Look, I don't rubbish your boy-friends. Please don't do it to mine,' Jo said sharply, stung by her sister's tone. 'And I'll spend the weekend with whoever I choose.'

'And you obviously choose not to spend it with me. Well, thanks a bunch. The only time I ask you to do something for me and you turn me down.'

'The only time?' Jo protested. Annabel could, and frequently did, twist people around her little finger. Especially Jo. 'That's not fair.'

'Sorry I wasted your precious time.' Annabel ignored Jo's attempt to interrupt. 'Have a nice weekend.'

'Annabel, please — ' Jo began. But the line was dead.

Jo frowned as she replaced the phone. It wasn't like Annabel to be quite so prickly, perhaps an indication of how worried she must be. Maybe she should think about putting Matt off and go with Annabel this weekend? She was obviously in quite a state.

Jo and Matt worked for the same law firm where Matt was a trainee solicitor and Jo a legal secretary. They'd been going out together since the firm's Christmas party and the weekend in the New Forest had been Matt's suggestion. It would, he said, give their relationship a chance to develop away from the prying eyes and wagging tongues of the office gossips.

If she and Matt had a future together, one weekend wouldn't make any difference, would it? Annabel needed her. For the horrific motorway pile up which killed their father hadn't just robbed Annabel of her last surviving parent but her sense of identity as well. The discovery that she'd been adopted had devastated them both and Jo well understood and sympathised with her sister's desperate need to find her birth mother.

Jo took a deep breath and picked up the phone.

As she waited for Matt to answer, she reached into her drawer, took out a bar of dark chocolate and broke off two squares. Would Matt be furious? Or just disappointed? Probably both. Her heart sank at the thought. In the couple of months she'd known him, she'd found out Matt didn't handle disappointment too well.

But, if she was honest, it wasn't only Annabel's call that had created doubts in Jo's mind about the coming weekend. As the bitter sweetness of the chocolate melted on her tongue, she acknowledged that all afternoon a sense of uneasiness had been building up inside her like the rain clouds that had been gathering outside the window.

'Matt? It's Jo here.' She swallowed the last of the chocolate hastily as he answered.

'I'd recognise that sexy voice anywhere.' He gave a soft, sensuous laugh. 'Do you have any idea what those husky tones do to me?'

'Don't, please,' she murmured.

'I've made you blush again, haven't I?' He chuckled. 'That's the other thing about you that turns me on. It's a long time since I met a girl who blushes. Just wait until tonight. Looking forward to it?'

'Actually, that's what I'm calling about.'

'Believe it or not, I was about to call you. I'm almost finished here. Any chance you can get away earlier than 3.30?'

'I'm sorry. I'm afraid there's been a problem.'

'A problem?' It was like the sun going in as the smile in his voice shut off. 'I thought you said you'd cleared it with Tim to leave early? It's going to make the driving hellish if we leave any later. Do you want me to have a word — ?'

'No. No. It's not that. Tim was fine about it. It's just that I don't think I can make it at all. Annabel needs me to — '

'Annabel?' His voice rose several shocked decibels. 'You're standing me up for your sister?'

'I'm not standing you up. Well, not in the way you mean. I'm really sorry, Matt. I hate letting you down like this but I can't make it this weekend. Annabel's been through such a lot lately that I really need to be with her when she — '

'Correct me if I'm wrong, Jo, but

didn't you tell me that Annabel is older than you?'

'By thirteen months. She's twenty five.' Jo fingered the fine gold chain around her neck, as the tone of his voice changed from honeyed sweetness to pure snarl. 'Why?' she asked.

'Don't you think she's old enough to sort out her own problems by now, without little sister holding her hand?'

'It's not a question of holding her hand. She's had a really tough time since Dad died and she needs me. And I'll be honest with you, Matt, I'm having second thoughts anyway.'

'Second thoughts? About me?'

His remarks about Annabel had stung and made saying what had to be said easier than she'd anticipated. 'We've only known each other four weeks and spending a weekend together . . . well, I don't think I'm ready to make that sort of commitment yet.'

'Commitment?' His laugh rang out. But there was no humour in it, only cruel, stinging mockery. 'Who said anything about commitment?' He enunciated each syllable of the word with exaggerated precision, then laughed again. 'You're getting ahead of yourself there, sweetie.'

'No, but — ' Jo's worrying fingers had moved from the chain at her neck to the fastener of her bag which suddenly gave way, showering the contents across her desk.

'A fun weekend. No strings. No regrets. That's all that was on offer. Now, if you're not interested, if it's more important to baby-sit your sister, then fine. Plenty of others I can call who'd jump at the chance.'

'Matt, I'm sorry. Perhaps we could meet up one day next week?'

'And give you the chance to stand me up again? Nobody, but nobody, does that to me twice. So thanks, but no thanks.'

For the second time in almost as many minutes Jo was left listening to the purr of the dialling tone telling her she'd been disconnected.

She put the phone down slowly and scooped her scattered possessions back in to her bag, while she tried to rid her head of the ringing echo of Matt's cruel laughter.

But this time, not even the rest of the chocolate bar could do that for her.

★　★　★

Jo's shoulders ached, her eyes were gritty with tiredness and the chicken salad sandwich she'd just eaten had contained precious little salad and even less chicken.

Once again, she tried to get through to her sister's mobile. Once again, all she got was her recorded voice inviting her to leave a message.

'Hi Annabel. It's Jo again and I'm fed up leaving messages you never pick up. What's the point of that fancy phone of yours if you don't switch the damn thing on?

'It's 7pm and I'm at Sedgemoor Services on the M5. As you may have gathered, I've changed my mind about the weekend. I'd love to come with you to Neston Parva tomorrow.

'It's taken hours to track you down. I phoned every hotel in Wells before I found the one you're in. Anyway, I've booked myself a room there. It's right across the landing from you, according to the lady I spoke to. So I'll see you there soon.

'This same lady says it's another hour's drive from here to Wells. I hope she's wrong because I'm really tired. It's been a nightmare drive, rain most of the way and all I want right now is a large gin and tonic and a long, hot bath. So — ' she hesitated, 'I'm sorry if I sounded a bit . . . well, less than enthusiastic earlier. It's not that I . . . well, you know . . . It's no good. I hate these damned machines. I'll talk to you later. Bye.'

* * *

Unfortunately, the receptionist had been right. It was almost exactly an hour later when Jo drove past the

16

Market Place and down Wells' High Street to the Black Lion Hotel. A larger than life black lion, his huge head resting on his paws, looked out from his vantage point on the roof of the entrance porch down on to the High Street.

It was like any other main street in any other small town, except for the channels of water that ran down either side of the road and the honey-coloured cathedral that sat in floodlit splendour.

The young woman behind the desk peered out at Jo from behind a fringe of long black hair that covered half her face. Her skin was unnaturally white and her eyes were so heavily ringed with black eyeliner she reminded Jo of a seriously undernourished panda.

'Hello, my name is Jo Frankley.' Jo dropped her bags at her feet and flexed her stiff shoulder muscles. 'My sister, Annabel Frankley is staying here and when I phoned earlier, you very kindly gave me a room near hers. I'll just check in and then can you tell her I'm here, please.'

The woman, whose name, according to the badge on her lapel, was Nikki, dropped her pen on the floor and with a muttered 'excuse me' bent down to retrieve it. After what seemed an age to Jo, she reappeared, peered at the computer screen and frowned.

'Did you say Frankley? Only there doesn't appear to be anyone booked in with that name.'

'But there must be. I only spoke to you an hour ago. Surely you remember?' Jo dragged her fingers through her hair, which felt in desperate need of a shampoo. 'You said a room was available across the landing from my sister.'

'Your sister?' Nikki echoed with a blank stare, while her long silver earrings glinted in the light as she bent forward to peer again at the screen.

'Annabel Frankley,' Jo repeated, forcing herself to remain calm and not let her rising irritation show. Right now, this girl was the only obstacle between her aching shoulders and that much needed hot bath. 'She's staying here, right? I phoned an hour ago and booked a room, just across the corridor from hers.'

'I'm sorry,' Nikki said as she shrugged her thin shoulders. 'I don't know who you spoke to but I'm afraid, not only is there no reservation in your name here, there isn't one for an Annabel Frankley either. Your sister is definitely not staying at this hotel.'

Jo stared, wide-eyed, at her. 'But when I spoke to you earlier, you said — '

'I said nothing.' Nikki spoke sharply, her face flushed under her too pale make-up. 'I've no idea what happened unless — well, it's just occurred to me. Are you sure you've got the right hotel? You'd be amazed how many times people do that, phone one hotel and turn up at another.'

'What?'

'I said, are you sure you've got the right hotel?'

'Yes. I heard you. It's just . . . ' Jo began to have a really, really bad feeling that started in the pit of her stomach but was now spreading around the rest of her body. 'The right hotel? But of course I have. I must have. Look, if it wasn't you I spoke to earlier, why don't you ask whoever was on reception at that time?'

'That's what I'm trying to tell you.' Her panda eyes looked straight into Jo's. 'I've been on reception since four o'clock this afternoon. I'm afraid there's no doubt. You've got the wrong hotel.'

2

'No. Oh, please, no.' Jo shook her head. What a stupid, stupid fool. The wrong hotel. She and Annabel would have a good laugh about it later but, at the moment, all she could think of was how tired she was.

Bone achingly, head swimmingly, brain numbingly tired.

'I'm so sorry to have made such a fuss. Of all the stupid things. Look, could I have a room for the night anyway?' she asked. 'I'm too tired to go searching around now. I'll catch up with my sister in the morning. I'll take any room. I don't care, just as long as it's got a bed and a bath.'

'I'm sorry.' Nikki shook her head again, sending the silver earrings swaying like metronomes. 'We're completely full. For the entire weekend.'

'Full?' Jo hadn't expected that, not in

the middle of January. 'Is there anywhere else in Wells that will have rooms?'

Another earring swinging shrug. 'You could try the Crown, up in the Market Place,' she said. 'It's across the road and up a little on the left. But you're in the one way system so you'll have to drive out of here, turn right, on to the relief road then follow the signs for the Cathedral. That'll bring you back to the Market Place.'

Relief road? The way Jo's day was going, she'd probably end up back on the motorway. No way was she getting back in that damn car tonight. It could stay in the Black Lion car park and if they didn't like it, tough. She'd sort it out in the morning.

She looked at her watch. It was just on eight-thirty. She could have been in the New Forest by now, sipping a gin and tonic in front of a roaring log fire. Instead, she was alone in a strange town with nowhere to stay and with a relationship that had taken one giant leap backwards.

Things didn't get much worse than that.

The Crown did indeed have a room, a charming one overlooking the Market Place and Cathedral. It had a low-beamed ceiling, an uneven floor which creaked a soft, almost musical murmur of protest at every movement and an exquisitely comfortable four-poster bed.

The longed for soak in a lavender-scented bath did much to ease her aching limbs and banish her brief, uncharacteristic moment of self pity. Instead, she was relieved she hadn't yet caught up with Annabel and was content to leave it until the morning.

Right now, the only thing she wanted to do was to curl up with her book in that beautiful bed that looked as if it had come straight out of the pages of a fairytale.

* * *

Jo caught her breath as she opened her curtains the next morning, taking in the stunning view as she looked across the busy Market Place towards the Cathedral. Its walls, the colour of pale honey, appeared to glow, warm and golden, despite the haze of fine rain that glistened on the pavements and collected in small pools on the blue and white awnings of the market stalls laid out below her.

She sat at the dainty mahogany writing desk in front of the window, rummaged in her bag for her phone and instead came across the leaflet containing the list of hotels she'd picked up at Sedgemoor Services. Why hadn't she thought of it before? She'd worked her way through the list yesterday in her effort to find Annabel's hotel.

There were crosses against the first two numbers — one of which was the hotel she was staying in now — but against the third she'd written 'Yes!', underlined the name of the hotel and drawn a smiley face.

It was The Black Lion, High Street,

Wells, Somerset.

So she'd been right after all. She had called the Black Lion. She must have done. It was that receptionist, Nikki, who'd put doubts in her mind. But why would she do that?

And then she realised something that would put it beyond doubt. Why hadn't she thought of it sooner? Like, last night for instance? She'd made the call on her mobile phone which stored the numbers of her most recent calls so the calls made to the various hotels would be listed on it.

She eventually found her phone buried beneath the detritus of paper clips, old train tickets and beads from a broken necklace that cluttered the bottom of her bag. She turned it on and flicked through the last calls and there, at the top of the list, were the last three she'd made. All beginning with 01749, the prefix for Wells. She compared the numbers with those on the leaflet then checked again to be sure. But there was no doubt.

The last call she'd made had indeed been to the Black Lion. She hadn't called the wrong hotel. So why had that girl Nikki tried to convince her otherwise? And if she'd lied about that, had she also lied about Annabel not being there? It didn't make sense.

Jo hardly noticed the rain as she strode down Wells' High Street, dodging the crowds of Saturday morning shoppers. Normally, she'd do almost anything to avoid confrontation, but not this morning. She was determined to have it out with Nikki, demand to know why she'd looked her straight in the eye last night and told her she must have phoned the wrong hotel and that neither she nor her sister were booked in.

The questions ran round and round in her head. Why had Nikki lied? And where was Annabel?

'Can I help you?' The man behind the reception desk looked up and smiled. His eyes were the deep rich blue of a spring sky while his hair was black as midnight. It was a surprising but attractive combination and at any other time Jo would have responded to his open, friendly smile with one of her own.

But not this morning. Right now the only thing she could think of was Nikki and what she was going to say to her.

'I need to see Nikki please,' she said crisply. 'The receptionist that was on duty last night.'

'I'm afraid she won't be in until this afternoon. Can I help you?'

Of course. Hotel staff worked shifts. Of course Nikki wouldn't still be on duty this morning. How stupid of her not to have realised that.

'Can you tell me if my sister's staying here please?' she asked. 'Her name's Annabel Frankley and I believe she arrived some time yesterday.'

He tapped at the keyboard then focussed on the screen in front of him. 'She is indeed. Would you like me to tell her you're here?'

Jo nodded as a wave of relief surged through her.

As she waited for him to put the call through, her mobile phone rang somewhere deep inside her bag.

'I left a message for her to ring. This could be her now,' she said as she scrabbled for the phone that was, as usual, buried at the bottom. In her anxiety to get to it before the caller rang off, she emptied the contents, item by item on to a nearby table.

The pile included the inevitable chocolate bar that she never went anywhere without, a packet of photographs and the office stapler which she must have swept into her bag by mistake after her run-in with Matt.

She became aware of the slight twitch of the man's strong, dark eyebrow as he watched her, which extended to a double twitch when she took out the fluorescent pink catnip mouse she'd bought for her elderly neighbour's new kitten.

When at last she found her phone, tangled around a spare pair of tights she'd thrown in her bag at the last minute, her embarrassment changed to anger as she saw it was Matt and not Annabel calling. She switched off the phone without taking the call and swept everything back in to her bag.

'I'm sorry,' he said, 'there's no reply from your sister's room. She could still be at breakfast or she may have already gone out.'

'Gone out?' Jo checked her watch. 'It's half past nine. That's the middle of the night for Annabel. And she never eats breakfast.'

'Or maybe she's in the bath, unless you're going to tell me she never takes a bath either?' His eyes, as they looked into hers, were smiling.

'She showers,' Jo said briefly, resisting the temptation to smile back at him. 'And now that we've established my sister is in fact staying here, can you explain why I was told last night that she was not?'

The smile in his eyes died as he frowned. 'I'm so sorry. There's obviously been a mistake. I'll — '

'Can you also explain,' she cut in, her voice as cold as a December dawn, 'why I was told there was no room available for me last night even though I'd phoned earlier to reserve one?'

His frown deepened. 'Is this why you wanted to see Nikki? Was it her you spoke to?'

Jo nodded. 'I'd like to speak to the Manager, please.'

'I am the Manager. My name is Rob Carlson. I promise you this will be fully investigated.'

'Right now, Mr Carlson, I'd prefer you investigate why my sister's not answering her phone.'

But Jo knew the answer, even before the woman he'd sent upstairs to check came back down, shaking her head. She always knew instinctively when Annabel was in trouble. She had done so since they were little and the feeling that something was wrong had been growing steadily all morning.

She heard the phone on the desk ring, saw him answer it then glance quickly in her direction.

'Okay, thank you, Anna,' he said, then turned to Jo. 'I'm afraid your sister's bed was not slept in last night. But don't look so anxious. There will be a perfectly reasonable explanation. Please don't worry.'

She gripped the strap of her shoulder bag so tightly, her fingernails left tiny crescent-shaped indentations in the soft leather. Just when she thought she'd found Annabel, this man was saying her bed hadn't been slept in and that nobody in the hotel had seen her since she'd checked in almost twenty four hours ago.

Then he went on to tell her not to worry? No chance.

'Should we call the police?' she asked.

Rob shook his head. 'Let's think this through first. You said your sister was expecting you?'

'Well, no, she wasn't exactly expecting me. I'd made arrangements to go away for the weekend. With a friend.

But it fell through at the last minute.' She swallowed hard. Would she ever be able to think of Matt without hearing his mocking laughter and recalling what a complete idiot she'd made of herself? She pushed the thought away and focussed on Annabel. 'So I came down here instead.'

'And your sister knew this?'

'She should have done. I left her loads of messages. But she's rubbish at picking them up.'

'Then, don't you think the most likely reason your sister didn't come back last night is nothing more sinister than she took a trip yesterday, it was further than she'd intended, so she decided to travel back today? Or maybe she met up with an old friend. Does she have friends in the area?'

'Not friends exactly, but yes.' Jo's anxiety eased slightly. Maybe Annabel had missed Jo's message last night to say she'd changed her mind about coming to Somerset. If so, it was possible she'd decided against waiting and had gone alone to meet her mother. It was also possible they'd got on so well, she'd been invited to stay the night.

'There is someone she may be with,' she admitted.

'Good.' Once again, he gave her his brilliant smile. 'Now that's cleared up, come into the residents' lounge. We'll have a coffee and discuss how to compensate you for yesterday's misunderstanding.'

'Compensate?' Jo flushed. Did he think that was why she'd complained? 'That won't be necessary, thank you. Look, I'm sorry I said anything. Please forget about it.' She turned to go. 'And you're right, of course. Annabel's probably staying with a friend.'

Then why was she still so jumpy? The small voice inside her head refused to go away. She wanted to accept Rob Carlson's perfectly reasonable explanation. And yet . . .

'At least have coffee with me. You look as if you could do with it.'

Before she could refuse, he took her

by the arm and led her into a small, oak-panelled room where golden chrysanthemums glowed in tall copper vases. The air was sweet with the fragrance of apple wood from the log fire that hissed and crackled in the ancient limestone hearth.

'I haven't had breakfast yet,' he went on, 'so you'd be doing me a favour by giving me an excuse for a break.'

His grin as he left to sort out the coffee forced Jo to revise her original estimate of his age from mid-thirties to mid-twenties. But what did his age matter? What was she doing here? In spite of her resolve to be more forceful, she'd fallen at the first hurdle. She didn't want to stay and have coffee with him, even though he was the most attractive man she'd met in a long time — and that included Matt — and the way his warm, appreciative smile lingered in his eyes helped smooth at least some of the dents Matt's cruel laughter had left in her self-esteem.

But she needed to be off, looking for

Annabel, otherwise the voice inside her head would give her no peace.

As she turned to go, she noticed a book that lay on the oak sideboard near the door. It was a slender paperback with a deep blue cover and the title *No Greater Love* embossed in fine gold lettering. She picked it up, intrigued by the sub title. 'The Story of Jacob Carlson,' she read aloud, 'Neston Manor's tragic hero. 1664–1685.'

Neston Manor. Could it be in the village of Neston Parva? Intrigued, she flicked the book open and began to read.

On the morning of the 16th September in the year of our Lord, 1685, Jacob Carlson prepared to meet his death on the scaffold. He was sorry for the grief this would cause his mother but comforted by the knowledge that his brothers and sisters would care for her in her sorrow. Jacob was at peace with his God and soon, Heaven be praised, he'd meet Him face to face, when he'd be rewarded for what he was about to do that day. He'd asked the Lord to be with him and, when the moment came, to give him the courage to meet his death bravely and quietly.

Jo shivered in spite of the warmth from the log fire and read on, intrigued by the opening page.

Before she could read much further, Rob came back with a tray of coffee and croissants which he placed on a low coffee table in front of the fire. She put the book on the table, sank into a squashy fireside chair and accepted the cup he held out to her.

The coffee was exactly how she liked it; hot, strong and aromatic. She was about to refuse the croissant when their warm, rich smell reached her nose. She couldn't resist.

'I've been reading the first pages of that book,' she managed to say between flaky, buttery mouthfuls. 'It sounds a fascinating story. Is Neston Manor anywhere near Neston Parva? Because that's where — ' She broke off suddenly, remembering in time her promise to Annabel not to tell anyone she'd tracked her birth mother to Neston Parva. 'I read about it somewhere,' she ended lamely.

'It's where it got its name from. The entire village was once part of the Neston Manor Estate, but that was a long, long time ago,' he said.

'Is it far from here? I'd love to see it.'

'You would?'

She laughed. 'Why so surprised? You sound as if — ' She broke off and looked again at the book's opening page. 'Jacob Carlson. The poor man who was about to die. And you're Rob Carlson. Is he an ancestor?'

'Apparently. And the reason I'm surprised you want to go there is because Neston Parva isn't exactly on the tourist trail, in spite of Caroline's best efforts.'

'Caroline?'

'Lady Caroline Staverton, of Neston Manor. She unearthed the story of Jacob Carlson and wrote it up.'

'So how did he die? It all sounds very intriguing.'

'He was hung. Or, to be completely accurate, the poor fellow was hung, drawn and quartered, as were many of the Duke of Monmouth's men following the rebellion of 1685. The poor chap was left strung up for weeks, apparently, as a lesson to others. Instant death to anyone who tried to cut him down.'

Jo shivered and moved closer to the fire. 'How terrible,' she murmured.

Rob shrugged and took a sip of coffee. 'They were hard, brutal times, that's for sure. But it was so long ago and the story may not even be true. If you ask me, Caroline's book has more to do with drumming up visitors to Neston Manor than historical accuracy.'

'The Manor's open to the public?' Jo was thankful to follow the conversation on to less gruesome ground.

'Only in the summer. However, if you're looking for places to visit today, Cheddar Gorge is spectacular any time and Wells itself is particularly good on a

Saturday because it's market day. And then, of course, there's Glastonbury or — '

'You sound as if you don't want me to go to Neston Parva. Why?'

'It's not that,' he assured her with a smile. 'But it's about as remote a place as you can get around here. And it's very easy to get lost out on the moors, especially on a day like today when visibility is poor and you can't get your bearings from landmarks.'

'The moors? There are moors in this part of Somerset? I never realised — but yes, of course, Sedgemoor.' Inside her head, something clicked. History had continued to fascinate her long after she left school. 'If I remember correctly, the Battle of Sedgemoor was around 1685. The last battle to be fought on English soil when James, Duke of Monmouth raised an army against the King. Then your ancestor, Jacob, was one of the Monmouth Rebels, which is why he was hanged by, I would imagine, the infamous Judge Jeffries. Is that right?'

'Ten out of ten. Although the battle site's not near here, but down towards Bridgwater. If you take my advice, you won't even try to find Neston Parva. It's nothing but a handful of houses, a church and a pub. Plus, of course, a couple of farms that at this time of the year turn the lanes around the village into a quagmire.'

'You're doing nothing to help Neston Manor's visitor numbers.' She smiled as she wiped the crumbs from her fingers then saw, with a flush of guilt that, in spite of saying she was not hungry, she'd just eaten two croissants. 'Perhaps I'll content myself with reading about it instead. Where can I buy a copy of this book?'

'You're welcome to that one. I keep a number in the hotel as a favour to my mother, who's a close friend of Caroline.'

'In that case, let me pay for it.'

'No, please take it — it's the least I can do. But a word of warning. Don't let Caroline Staverton beguile you into thinking Neston Parva is a more interesting place than it really is: She has a way with words and can conjure up a story out of nothing.' He smiled.

Jo immediately thought of Annabel, so much on her mind that even Rob's description of a complete stranger reminded her.

Her father used to say with exasperation and pride that Annabel could spin a story out of the air. Annabel's way with words, coupled with her ability to turn the smallest happening into a drama, had got the two girls into trouble on many occasions in spite of Jo's best efforts not to be drawn in.

Of course, that same talent had gone on to enable Annabel to fulfil her ambition to train as a journalist and even though she was still near the bottom of a very long ladder, Jo had no doubt she'd climb as high and as fast as she wished.

'I'm sorry?' She reddened as she realised Rob had said something and now expected a response from her. 'I'm afraid I was miles away.'

'I said the recent heavy rains have made the rhines brim full, which can be quite dangerous if you don't know the area.'

'What's a rhine?'

'The word is spelt r-h-i-n-e, like the German river but some pronounce it to rhyme with bean, depending on which part of the county you're from. It's a drainage ditch that criss-crosses the Somerset Levels. Without them, much of this part of Somerset from Glastonbury to Burnham-on-Sea and across to Bridgwater would be under water at this time of the year.'

'I see. But how can a ditch be dangerous?'

'These aren't ordinary ditches. Many run alongside the road and are unfenced. They have very steep sides and can be as much as six feet deep. Sheep and cattle have fallen in and drowned because they've been unable to get back up. Sadly, so too have people. Only last year a couple of lads stole a car and thought they'd take a shortcut across the moors in the dead of night. Their car skidded off the road and landed upside down in a rhine.' He shook his head. 'It was two days before they were eventually found.'

Fear clutched at Jo's heart. 'Annabel,' she whispered. 'You don't think she's had an accident?'

3

Strangers had never been welcome in Neston Parva but in the summer of 1685 after Monmouth's so-called Pitchfork Rebellion ended in failure, Judge Jeffries sent men to every West Country village to compile a list of those who were 'absent from their homes during the rebellion of James Scott, late Duke of Monmouth'. Reprisal was swift and bloody.

It was a time to settle old scores and grievances, a time when neighbour informed on neighbour and treachery was rife.

It was a time when strangers were not only unwelcome, they were feared and despised.

'You think your sister has ended up in a rhine? Is that what you're worried about?' Rob looked at her with troubled eyes. 'I thought we'd agreed she was

44

staying with friends? I wouldn't have said anything if I'd realised it would set your thoughts along that road. No, of course your sister hasn't ended up in a rhine. For a start, she'd have no reason to go out on the moors, would she?'

'No, of course not. No reason at all.' It took a huge effort to make her voice sound calm and level above the panicky rush of her heartbeat. 'Mr Carlson, you're a busy man and I've taken up enough of your time. Thanks for a lovely breakfast. I'll leave a note for Annabel at reception then remove my car from your car park. I left it there last night when I was too tired to tackle the relief road.'

'Very wise,' he said with a grin. 'People have been known to miss Wells altogether once they get on it. And my name is Rob, by the way.'

Jo smiled, thanked him then went out to her car. She took out the book about Neston Manor and turned to the section on the back marked 'How to get there' then set off to find Annabel.

* * *

The soft rain had given way to a relentless downpour as Jo turned off the main road and took the narrow, willow-fringed road that led, ruler straight, across the moors to Neston Parva. What little landscape she could see through the driving rain was very different from the lush Somerset countryside she was familiar with. It was bleak, flat and empty with scrappy blackthorn hedges and few trees apart from the misshapen willows whose bare branches made her think of skeletal fingers clawing at the leaden sky.

As she approached one of the farms she assumed was responsible for the thick layer of mud that turned the road into a skating rink, a black and white collie with wild eyes rushed towards her, barking furiously at the car. Jo braked and felt the steering wheel go slack in her hands as she veered in to a skid.

When it stopped, the car was at right

angles to the road with both front wheels up on the grass verge. Trembling with shock, she got out and looked down at the sheer drop that was little more than two feet away from the front of her car.

So this, she thought with a shudder, was one of the rhines Rob had warned her about. She refused to admit, even to herself, that she wished she'd taken his advice and not come. Instead, she got back into the car, gave the collie who'd returned for a second onslaught a withering look, and drove on carefully towards the village.

Neston Parva was exactly as Rob had described it. A small, grey church with a square stubby tower, a pub with sludgy green, flaking paintwork and a few houses clustered around a triangle of patchy grass that didn't merit the title of village green.

Jo held her coat above her head to shield herself from the driving rain and got out to have a closer look at the noticeboard on the far side. Unlike the pub's paintwork, this was fresh and new and the gold lettering shone out against the dark blue background.

'The Great Neston Oak,' she read. 'This marks the spot where the Great Neston Oak once stood, from which brave Jacob Carlson was hung on 16th September, 1685. He went to his death rather than betray his friend, Sir Roger Staverton and this plaque is erected in grateful recognition of his sacrifice by Sir Peter Staverton, a direct descendant.'

It ended with the quotation Jo recognised. It was also the source of the title of the book Rob had given her. 'Greater love hath no man than he lay down his life for his friend'.

Intrigued, she promised herself she'd read more of the book as soon as she could. Then she smiled as she recalled Rob's cynical remark about the purpose of the book being to increase the Manor's visitor numbers, for close to the noticeboard, in the same tasteful blue and gold was a discreet but unmissable sign pointing to Neston Manor together with the opening dates and times.

Her eye followed the direction of the sign, then stopped abruptly as something the colour of bright English mustard shone through the curtain of heavy rain.

There was a small car park at the back of the church and there, parked neatly against the far wall was a yellow VW car. Like Annabel's.

As Jo got closer she saw from the registration number that it was, indeed, her sister's car. It was locked so Jo peered through the rain-streaked window. Annabel's blue and black raincoat was on the back seat while on the front passenger seat lay a notebook and her smart, new mobile phone.

Jo looked around at the cluster of houses, struck for the first time by an odd stillness that shrouded the village. Where was everyone?

But more important, where was Annabel?

She listened, straining her ears for the sound of her voice or her sudden, distinctive peal of laughter. But there was nothing. Only the sound of the rain bouncing off the roof of Annabel's car and the drone of a tractor as it made its sluggish way across a distant, rain-soaked field.

'Annabel?' Her voice rang out across the silence. But nobody answered. No heads appeared at windows, or lace curtains twitched as occupants peered to see who was disturbing the unnatural silence.

'Annabel?' she called louder this time. But the only response came from a clump of tall beech trees behind the church, where rooks busied themselves in the tangle of top branches. They mocked her with calls of their own as they wheeled against the grey sky like black plastic bags tossed on the wind.

Jo looked back inside the car at her sister's phone left carelessly on the front passenger seat and the bad feeling that had been plaguing her all morning suddenly got a whole heap worse.

Annabel never went anywhere without her precious phone. Jo was always teasing her about it, saying that it was an extension of her right hand.

So where was she?

Jo set off on foot, determined to find her sister. If Annabel's car with her notebook and mobile phone was here, then she couldn't be far away. And as Rob Carlson had been quite accurate in his assertion that Neston Parva was nothing more than a church, a pub and a few houses, it shouldn't take too long to check.

Even if she had to knock on every single door in the village, she was going to find her sister. Then, and only then, would she relax.

She walked across to the pub. The Staverton Arms looked even more run down close up. Flakes of the sludgy green paint from the front door lay scattered across the doorstep like fallen leaves while a single hanging basket hung forlornly alongside, its solitary occupant, once a leggy geranium, now desiccated by winter frosts.

She opened the door and paused at the entrance while her eyes adjusted to the gloom. The low-ceilinged bar was empty except for two men who huddled close to an ineffectual coal fire that belched out a cloud of acrid smoke as Jo closed the door behind her.

The men stopped talking and turned to watch her as she walked up to the bar, her heels tapping a hollow rhythm on the bare floor.

The sour smell of hot, stale fat drifted across from a glass-fronted warming cupboard at the far end of the bar, where two sausage rolls and a dubious looking pie sweated under the yellow light.

'Hello?' she called, then turned to the two men. 'Is anyone serving?'

The younger man stood up. His thick black hair curled over the collar of his leather jacket. His dark eyes and prominent nose gave him a Mediterranean appearance, but when he spoke, his accent was the long, slow drawl that was pure Somerset.

'Poor old Ted's hard of hearing,' he said. 'You'll have to shout.' His leather jacket creaked as he sauntered up to the bar and stood beside her, so close Jo could smell the mixture of beer and tobacco on his breath. She moved aside as he leaned across the bar and shouted, 'Ted? Shop.'

An old man, stooping and gaunt, his neck as thin and scrawny as a turkey's, shuffled in to the bar. Jo ordered a mineral water and immediately wished she hadn't as he took for ever to shuffle up to the other end of the bar and reach up stiffly to take a bottle from the top shelf. When he returned with it, she hadn't the heart to point out that she had asked for mineral and not tonic water and decided not to push her luck by asking for ice and lemon as well.

'I'm wondering if my sister has been in here, either today or yesterday?' she asked as she handed him the money, careful to enunciate each word as clearly as she could.

'Your sister? No, no, no.' He shook his head, the action reminding Jo even more forcefully of a turkey. 'Not in here. No. No. Definitely not.'

'But how do you know? I haven't told you what she looks like yet.'

'It makes no difference. I know because there've been no strangers in here, male or female since . . . let me see now,' his faded blue eyes looked up at the ceiling, as if the answer was written there, 'since Boxing Day lunchtime, I reckon.'

Jo turned to the two men who were watching her with undisguised curiosity. 'Did either of you see her? She's in her early twenties, long dark hair, about five foot seven, slim — '

'You heard what Ted said,' the younger man interrupted. 'There's been no strangers in here, male or female. Especially not female. I'd have remembered a slim young female with long dark hair, that's for sure.' With a sideways look at his grinning companion, he winked and took a long pull of his beer.

'But I've just seen her car,' Jo said. 'In the car park behind the church. Do you have any idea where she might be?'

He shrugged. 'Interested in old churches, is she? Only I don't think ours is anything special.'

'No. She's not. She's — look, hang on, I've got a picture of her somewhere. Maybe this'll help.'

She didn't usually carry photographs with her but she'd put some in her bag on Friday morning to show Matt. She flipped through the photographs, hurrying past the ones of Matt until she came to several shots of Annabel she'd taken at Christmas. She selected one and handed it to Ted.

'Look. That's my sister. She — '

'Well, I'm damned,' he muttered, leaning forward to get a closer look.

'You see? You have seen her.' She'd caught the flash of recognition in the old man's eyes.

'Well, if she isn't a dead ringer — '

'Now there's no need to go frightening the maid, Ted.' The older man came up to the bar and took Annabel's photograph from Ted.

'What do you mean?' she demanded as the rest of the photographs slipped from her fingers and pattered, unheeded, on to the floor.

He had the same hooked nose, the same dark hair, although not so much of it, as the younger man. His father? Probably. Certainly both men had the same suspicious, menacing look in their dark, gipsy eyes.

Did she mean menacing? Was she allowing her imagination to run away with her a bit here? This sort of dramatic overreaction was Annabel's territory, not hers. Nevertheless, Jo stepped back, her foot slipping on one of the fallen photographs as she did so.

'Look, Ted, why don't you go and check the barrel?' he said. 'I said earlier I didn't think that last pint you pulled was quite right, didn't I? Go on. I'll mind the bar for you.'

'I'll have you know there's nothing wrong with my beer, Seth Carlson,' Ted began, his face reddening. 'And I didn't mean — '

'Of course you didn't mean to frighten the maid. Don't worry about it. You just worry about that barrel.'

Ted shuffled out, still muttering to himself.

Jo wanted to call after him, to ask him not to leave her alone with the two men who were watching her intently.

Jo took a deep, steadying breath then turned to face them across the gloomy, smoke-filled room. They knew something about her missing sister. She was sure of it.

'What did he mean?' she asked, forcing herself to meet the older man's challenging gaze. 'A dead ringer for who?'

'There now. Do you see what I mean, Jay, about upsetting people without meaning to?' Seth cut across her question and turned to his son. 'Old Ted uses a casual expression, maybe not known to the maid here — and she, being in a highly nervous state, jumps to the wrong conclusion.'

'I am not in a highly nervous state, as you put it,' Jo said firmly. 'Ted recognised Annabel. I'm sure he did. I saw it in his eyes. I also know what 'dead ringer' means. I want to know who he thought she was like.'

Jo was convinced the old man had either recognised Annabel or her picture had reminded him of someone. Was it someone here in Neston Parva? The someone Annabel had come all this way to see? Her birth mother? It had to be.

Jo was convinced if she could find her, whoever she was, she'd find Annabel too. She had no choice — if she wanted to question Ted further she had to stay here and face Seth out, much as she wanted to run away.

She squared her shoulders, stuck her hands in her pockets so he wouldn't see how badly they were shaking and forced herself to look him in the eye. For what could only have been a fraction of a second, but felt like for ever, nobody spoke. The only sound was the loud tick of an enormous white and black clock that would have been more at home on a station platform than behind a bar.

'Who is it?' she asked defiantly.

Jo held Seth's gaze and felt a surge of triumph when he looked away. Then he gave a sudden laugh and shook his head. 'That Ted. He's a case, isn't he? Should have been pensioned off years ago. Only keeps his job because Peter took pity on him when his wife died. Told him he had a job for life and — '

'Who is it?' Jo repeated the question with the same quiet emphasis, convinced now that Seth was covering up for someone.

'Judy Garland.'

'What?' Behind her, she heard Jay snigger, but she held Seth's gaze.

He picked up the photo again, looked at it and grinned. Whatever weakness Jo thought she'd detected in his eyes had vanished.

'Judy Garland,' he repeated. 'And do you know, I think Jay's right. Your sister definitely has a look of Judy about her. Course, you're too young to remember her but Ted's a huge fan. Seen all her films.'

Jo shook her head, aware that the moment, whatever it was, wherever it may have led, had passed.

'Here, Jay, you pop down to the cellar and make sure old Ted hasn't fallen down the steps or anything nasty.'

'But, Dad, I'd better — '

'You'll do as I say,' Seth snapped. 'Go and help Ted.'

Jo watched the younger man slouch off, muttering to himself as he went.

'Very considerate of you,' she said, her voice ice-tipped with sarcasm.

Seth leaned against the bar. This time his smile did reach his eyes. 'That's how we are in Neston Parva. Neighbourly. When you live out in the sticks like we do, folk have to look out for each other. It's how we've always done it.'

He moved towards her. Jo stepped

back, the corner of the bar jabbing her in the back as she did so. But he didn't touch her. Instead, he bent down and picked up the scattered photographs.

'This your man? You make a nice looking couple.' He tapped a oil ingrained finger at the photograph on the top of the pile. It was one of her and Matt, arms wrapped around each other, faces touching, laughing into the camera.

'Why don't you go back to him? Back where you belong. There's nothing for you here. Or your sister. You tell her that when you catch up with her. There's nothing here for her. Nothing at all.' He leaned towards her, the smell of engine oil clinging to his clothes as his dark gipsy eyes bored into hers. 'That's meant as a bit of friendly advice. Nothing more.'

Jo faced him across the dim bar, her heart banging against her ribcage, her breathing shallow. She wanted to challenge him, to demand what gave him the right to tell her to leave Neston

Parva and what he meant by saying there was nothing here for Annabel?

But the small burst of courage that had enabled her to stand up to him a few minutes ago was no match against his barely veiled threat.

She flinched as his hand went towards his pocket. He took out a packet of cigarettes and lit one, cupping his hand over the flame, watching her intently as he did so. Then he glanced across at the 'no smoking' sign and laughed softly.

He'd won. And he knew it.

4

A blast of cold air caused the fire to belch out another acrid cloud as the outside door opened and she heard, with relief, the sounds of someone coming in. Only then did she realise how long she'd been holding her breath. She gripped the threadbare seat of the nearest bar stool as her legs threatened to buckle beneath her.

Seth flicked his cigarette into the fire, placed the photos on the bar beside her then turned to face the man who'd come in. Jo stuffed the photos into her handbag and was about to leave when she, too, recognised the newcomer.

'Afternoon, Rob,' Seth said. 'Not working today?'

Rob Carlson shook droplets of rain from his blue Gore-Tex jacket. 'Not this afternoon, Seth. My day for — ' He stopped as he noticed Jo for the first time and it took a few seconds for his natural good manners to overcome his astonishment. 'Good afternoon, Miss Frankley. You decided not to take my advice, I see. But maybe you'll appreciate, from the shocking state of the roads out here, why I said what I did.'

'I was fine,' she said, trying not to think back to her stomach churning skid near the entrance to the farm. Her chin came up as, thanks to his presence, she began to recover some of her composure. 'At least, I was until just now.'

'And I was just saying the same as you,' Seth cut in. 'I was telling her how dangerous the roads around here can be at this time of year. Just giving you a bit of friendly advice, wasn't I?'

But before Jo could respond Ted returned, his narrow face transformed by a smile of genuine welcome. 'Rob. Good to see you, lad. Your usual?' Without waiting for an answer, he pulled a pint and placed it on the counter. 'Saw your mother earlier, out with the dogs. She's looking better now she's shaken off that bout of flu.'

Rob nodded. 'She's fine now. But you know what she's like. Independent as ever.'

'You live here?' Jo's face darkened as she turned on Rob.

'My mother does,' he said. 'I have a flat in Wells.'

Wild thoughts raged through her mind like an autumn gale. Was he in on this conspiracy surrounding Annabel? Certainly he'd tried hard to dissuade her from coming to Neston Parva this morning. And he hadn't looked at all pleased to see her here. So, had he been summoned, like the cavalry? Was that why Jay slipped away? Had Rob come all this way to persuade her to go back to Wells?

She was surprised at the depth of her disappointment, as if she'd been let down by an old and dear friend. But why should she feel like that? She'd only met Rob this morning and although he'd been charmingly attentive, he'd merely been doing his job. She had no reason to think of him as a friend. No reason at all to feel let down by him.

'I found my sister's car,' she said. 'By the church. I was asking this . . . ' she paused and chose the next word with care, letting sarcasm sharpen her tone, 'this gentleman here if he knew anything about it when you came in.'

'And this 'gentleman' told you he didn't,' Seth growled. 'It's probably just a car that's the same make and model as your sister's. What sort does she drive?'

'A yellow VW beetle. It's quite distinctive but even if it wasn't, I do know my own sister's registration number. Look, I've wasted enough time in here. She's here somewhere and I'm going to find her.'

Rob replaced his pint on the bar. 'Keep this warm for me, Ted.' Then he turned to Jo. 'I think perhaps you'd better show me.'

Jo was happy to leave the oppressive atmosphere of the pub as they walked across to the church. 'Perhaps now you'll take my worries about Annabel seriously,' she said, as she hurried to keep up with Rob's long, loping strides.

'I always took them seriously.'

'My sister's car could have been there all night. Well, see for yourself.'

They came through the small lane that led to the church. Jo stopped so abruptly Rob almost collided with her.

The car park was empty. Annabel's car had vanished.

Jo stared at the space where the yellow VW should have been. She blinked hard, as if by doing so she could make it reappear.

'But it was here.' She raked her fingers through her hair. 'I saw it not ten minutes ago. You must believe me.'

'But as Seth says, it's a popular make.'

'And Seth also said that — ' Jo stopped suddenly as a connection she should have made a while ago finally clunked in to place. How could she have been so stupid not to have seen it sooner? 'The man in the pub. Seth. I've just realised. His surname — it's the same as yours. The old man called him Seth Carlson.'

A puzzled frown creased Rob's strong brow. 'Well, yes. He would. That's his name.'

'Is he — are you related?'

'He's my uncle, my father's brother as a matter of fact. But what's this all about? Did Seth say something to upset you? I know he's a bit of a rough diamond and can be an awkward so-and-so at times, but his heart's in the right place. There's no harm in him.'

'Looking out for each other,' she murmured.

'I'm sorry? I'm afraid I don't follow.'

'That's what he told me. He said folks in these parts look out for each other, same as they've always done.'

'Well, of course they do. This is a small community where everyone knows everyone else. At least they used to before the weekenders bought up all the houses and pushed the property prices beyond the reach of most of the locals, particularly the young ones. But that's the way it is in many rural areas these days. However, if Seth said anything to upset you, I'll have it out with him and he'll apologise, I promise you.'

Jo shook her head. 'Don't bother,' she said. 'It was nothing. But there is something you can do for me. If it's true and everyone knows everyone else, does this photograph remind you of anyone? The barman certainly seemed to think so.'

She passed him the same picture she'd shown to Ted. Rob looked at it carefully for a while then passed it back to her, shaking his head.

'I'm sorry. It doesn't, I'm afraid. But if she's one of the weekenders, then I wouldn't.'

Jo remembered her promise to Annabel. Was this, she wondered, the time to break it? Then she remembered she was talking to the nephew of Seth Carlson, the man who'd threatened her

was parked over by the church until a few moments ago. You didn't happen to see it leave, did you?'

'I'm sorry, I didn't,' she said, before adding, 'at least, not properly. I was in the kitchen preparing lunch when I heard a car start up, but by the time I looked up, all I saw was a car — a yellow one, as you said — disappearing around the corner.'

'Did you see the car arrive? And did you see which way it went?' Jo asked anxiously.

'I was visiting a friend in Bath all day yesterday but the car was in the church car park when I got back at five o'clock. As to which direction your sister took, I'm pretty sure she turned left by the green and went back towards Wells.'

'That's great. Thank you for your help. I'm sorry to have troubled you and I'll let you get on with your lunch.' Jo was very conscious of the appetising smell of roast lamb with, she thought, garlic and rosemary that drifted towards her. 'With a bit of luck, I'll catch up with her back in Wells.'

But in spite of her desire to catch up with Annabel as soon as possible and to leave the strange, claustrophobic little village behind her, Jo drove slowly out of the village and on to the moors, conscious more than ever of the rhines on both sides of the mud-covered single track road.

She'd not gone very far when her phone rang. It had to be Annabel, surely? Light-headed with relief, she pulled in to a nearby gateway, took out her phone and checked the caller ID.

Her relief vanished as she saw Matt's name on the screen. She switched the phone off. She had neither the time nor the inclination to deal with him at the moment.

She'd stopped the car at a point where the road took yet another abrupt right-angled turn, one of the things that made driving these moorland roads so difficult. As she leaned across to pick up her bag which had fallen on to the floor she noticed that the grass verge ahead had two parallel ruts gouged deep into its rain sodden surface.

A small thicket of hazel and hawthorn formed a natural shelter for the stocky brown and white cattle that grazed the field. But instead, the herd was at the far end, huddled together in a tight, uneasy group. Jo wondered what had spooked them. Maybe the wild eyed collie she'd met earlier.

Then she saw it. A glimpse of mustard yellow through the broken and bare hawthorn branches.

'No. Dear God, no. Don't let it be — ' Her mind racing, Jo got out of the car and ran to the edge of the rhine.

Annabel's car was nose down in the brackish water, rear tyres pointing skyward, the car's underbelly exposed. Around it, as if in a giant's cauldron, bubbles large and small broke the surface of the water while the air was thick with the stench of newly disturbed stagnant mud.

'Annabel,' she screamed. 'Can you hear me?'

But the only response came from the

rooks, wheeling about in the air above a line of tall sycamores, scolding her loudly for disturbing the still of the afternoon.

She ran to the edge of the rhine. 'Annabel! Annabel. Can you hear me?' she cried.

She tried desperately to see inside the car but it was hopeless. She recalled Rob's stories about submerged cars, drowned people and cattle with terrifying clarity and was just about to launch herself down the steep, near vertical bank when she heard a car approaching.

'Stop. Please stop.' She ran towards it, her arms waving wildly. 'Please help me.'

She was in such a state of panic, it didn't occur to her to be surprised that the driver turned out to be Rob, whom she'd left not ten minutes earlier about to sit down to lunch with his mother.

He jumped out of his car and sprinted towards her. 'What is it? What's wrong, Jo?'

'It's Annabel. Her car. It's down in there.' Her frantic words tumbled over each other as she ran back towards the edge of the rhine. 'Hurry. For pity's sake, please hurry.'

Rob ran across, peered down, then grabbing the branch of an overhanging willow tree for support, he slithered down the bank. She heard his quick intake of breath as he entered the icy water.

As he touched the car, Jo gave a cry as it moved and slid further in, sending up another ferment of bubbles. Rob jumped out of the way and heaved himself back up the bank, the water dripping off him.

'Don't leave her,' Jo cried. 'Please don't leave her down there.'

'I'm not but I couldn't reach the door, not without letting go of the branch,' he said, his breath coming in short gasps. 'There's quite an undertow from the car which is still sinking. But I'm pretty sure there's no one in the car. But the whole thing is very unstable.'

Jo grabbed his arm. 'Pretty sure? You're only pretty sure she's not in there? But she might be. I'm sorry, I can't just stand here — look, hold on to me while I go down.'

'No, it's not safe. Do you have a phone?'

She nodded. 'It's in the car.'

'Good, then you go and dial nine nine nine while I fetch the tow rope from my car. I'll see if I can get a line to it. Now go on, hurry. And tell them it's just outside Neston Parva, on the Wells road, near Longmoor Farm.'

Jo's hands were shaking so badly she could hardly punch the small buttons of her phone.

Hurry, hurry, she repeated silently as she waited for them to answer: *For pity's sake, hurry.*

After what seemed to her fevered brain like an eternity her call was eventually answered.

As she was making the call, a car came along and, seeing the road blocked by Rob's car, stopped to help. A few minutes later another car joined them.

The next hour passed in a confusion of frantic action — or was it minutes? Ten? Twenty? Thirty?

Looking back on it later, Jo couldn't be sure as everything became a blur of noise and activity.

She could only stand, her back against her car, arms hugging her body, watching, praying as Annabel's car was eventually dragged, dripping and creaking, from the brackish water. The noise sent the group of cattle, which had edged forward as their curiosity got the better of them, stampeding for the safety of the far end of the field again.

As the car was towed out, Jo looked down into the rhine, where the water had taken on the consistency of double cream, the colour of peat and the odour of hell itself.

She shuddered and asked herself the question she'd been asking over and over.

'Annabel,' she whispered. 'Please, no.'

5

There was the touch of a hand on her shoulder and she whirled round, half expecting to see Annabel standing there, dripping wet, but safe and well. But it was only Rob, his face full of concern as he looked at her.

'Have they . . . found her?' She forced herself to ask the question. 'Was she inside?'

'Jo. Come away from the edge.' He took her hand gently and led her towards her car. Then, he placed both hands on her shoulders and turned her to face him. 'Listen to me, Jo. I was right. Annabel wasn't in the car. She never had been.'

'But I don't understand . . . ' Jo shook her head, bewildered.

'The police are sure it had been pushed in the rhine deliberately,' Rob said, his hands still resting on her shoulders. 'It's a favourite spot for dumping things, one of the few places around here where the water's deep enough. Only someone else had had the same idea and an old gate was stopping the car from being completely submerged. That's what I was standing on when I went down to look.'

'Then Annabel isn't — she wasn't — ' Jo's legs almost gave way beneath her as relief turned her knees to jelly. She stumbled slightly and Rob's arms tightened around her, pulling her closer into him.

'She wasn't in the car,' Rob repeated softly, his breath warm on the top of her head.

'Oh, thank goodness. Thank goodness,' she breathed. 'But I don't get it. She'd never do a thing like that. She loves that car. It doesn't make any sense at all.'

'Who says it was Annabel?'

'Your mother. She said she'd seen Annabel drive away. Then ten minutes after telling me that, I find Annabel's car, nose down in filthy brown water.'

Her relief was short-lived as another, horrible thought occurred to her and she pulled away from Rob, her eyes swimming with tears. 'Poor Bel, she must have tried to swim for it and got swept away. Or . . . ' Her voice cracked and she pulled away from him and looked around wildly. 'M-maybe she got sucked down into the mud. Where have the police gone? Why aren't they sending divers down?'

'Jo, listen to me.' Rob took her hands firmly in his. 'The car was empty when it went in to the rhine. If anyone had been in it at the time and managed to get out, then either a door or a window would have been open. And they weren't.'

'Yes, but . . . '

'And, what's even more significant, there were no keys in the ignition. Think about it — you're in a rapidly submerging car, you're hardly likely to take the keys out of the ignition before you bail out, are you? I promise you there was no one in the car when it

81

went in to the rhine. It was pushed in. Do you understand what I'm saying? There was no one in the car.'

'But your mother saw her.'

'My mother saw Annabel's car being driven away. She only got the merest glimpse of who was driving it. After you left, she began to think about it and the more she thought, the stronger her impression that it had been a man, not a woman, at the wheel. That was why she sent me after you. And thank goodness she did.'

'A man? She was sure it was a man driving the car?'

'As sure as she could be. It was only a glimpse.'

This time, Jo's relief was total. This time, she allowed herself to believe it. Annabel hadn't been in the car when it slid in to the rhine. She wasn't lying down there, somewhere in that thick, brown gloopy water. Gradually, her heartbeat returned to normal and she became aware of her surroundings. She became aware, too, that Rob was still holding both her hands — and that his were cold. Very, very cold.

'Your hands. Oh, Rob, they're like blocks of ice,' she exclaimed. 'And your clothes. They're soaked. You must be frozen.'

'I've been warmer,' he said with a wry grin. 'It's got something to do with paddling around in a rhine on a January afternoon. But it could have been worse. I took my jacket off before going in, so at least that's still reasonably dry and clean.'

'What can I say? I feel terrible now about asking you to do it.' She pushed her hand through her hair. 'Especially as it was all for nothing. But I was so sure.'

'That's all right, Jo. Believe me, I'm just very, very thankful it was all for nothing in the end.'

'So am I.' She blinked back the tears that scalded the insides of her eyelids. 'Oh, so am I. You'll never know how much. I don't know how to begin to thank you. I'm so very grateful to you.

It could all have been so very different.' She swallowed hard, took a deep breath and regained control. 'Now, go back to your mother's. I'll be fine now, thanks. You'd better get changed out of those wet things.'

'I'm going back there now. I've phoned her to let her know what's happened and I'm under strict orders to bring you back with me.'

'But I've got to talk to the police. They drove off before I had chance to speak to them properly. I wanted to know if they had any idea who did this.'

'I've already spoken to them. They say they've got a few ideas about who's responsible but wouldn't go into details. As for telling them about Annabel being missing — I would hold fire on that one for a while. She'll be pretty embarrassed if you've sent the police to hunt her down when all the time she's been off shopping for the day, won't she?' He went across to his car and opened the passenger door for her. 'Come on, get in. I'll drive you back to my mother's.'

'But I can't.'

'And I can't go back without you,' he said with a smile. 'Don't be deceived by her gentle looks. My mother is definitely in the she-who-must-be-obeyed category. Besides, I told the police that was where you were going to be for the next couple of hours, in case they want to talk to you again, which, incidentally, they thought was unlikely. So come on. You can leave your car here and pick it up later.'

'No, I'll drive it.' The thought of leaving her car next to the place where Annabel's went in was too horrible to contemplate. 'I will come back to your mother's house, though. And thank you.' She fought to keep the tremor out of her voice as she struggled once again to express feelings that came from a place so deep inside her. There were no adequate words. 'I don't know how to thank you for what you . . . I'll never forget what you did . . . what you tried to do for me — and Annabel — back there.'

'You can thank me by doing what my

mother says. Now come on,' he said. 'There's a hot shower and a very late lunch waiting. And, I don't know about you but I'm starving. Someone ate most of the croissants I'd planned to have for my breakfast this morning.'

She felt her cheeks redden with his gentle teasing. It was only this morning, but already seemed so long ago now.

As she followed him back into the village, Jo was surprised to find that she, too, was hungry. The first time she'd been properly hungry, as opposed to craving comfort food, since Matt had dumped her. Or had she dumped him? To her surprise, she found she didn't really care, one way or another.

There was nothing like facing up to the possibility of the death of a dearly loved sister to put everything else into perspective.

But Annabel had not died. And for that reason alone, Jo felt better than she'd done for twenty-four hours. Added to which, she had lamb roasted with garlic and rosemary to look forward to.

* * *

'That was a wonderful lunch, Mrs Carlson. Thank you so much.' Jo leaned back in the wicker chair and accepted the cup of coffee Rob handed to her with a smile of thanks.

'Please, call me Clare. And it was the least I could do after sending you off on a wild goose chase. I still feel terrible about that. If I'd only thought more carefully.'

'I'd have still gone,' Jo said. 'But if it wasn't Annabel driving the car, then who was it? And what were they doing with Annabel's car?'

Rob, his coffee making completed, joined Jo and his mother in the conservatory that looked out on to Clare's garden where bright yellow crocuses pushed through the grass like candle flames and a well-stocked bird table attracted a noisy group of sparrows and blue tits.

'I'm afraid car crime doesn't just happen in the big cities,' he said. 'We have our share of it in the country, too, more's the pity.'

'You mean you agree with the police?' Jo asked.

'That Annabel's car was stolen? Yes, of course I do. I also agree with them that Annabel will turn up safe and well. You said earlier your sister had no idea you were going to follow her down here and that you've been unable to contact her to let her know you're here. So she could be anywhere, unaware of your concern.'

'She's not anywhere. Annabel came to Neston Parva,' she said. 'I know she did. After all, that was why she came to Wells in the first place.' She stopped as she became aware that Clare and Rob were both watching her with undisguised curiosity.

'Why on earth would your sister choose to come to this God-forsaken place?' Rob questioned.

'Rob. Please,' Clare protested. 'It's not that bad.'

'Sorry . . . ' He grinned and raised a

hand in acknowledgement. ' . . . why would she come to this out-of-the-way village in the middle of winter? Did it not strike you how quiet it is here?'

Jo remembered the strange, uncanny silence she'd felt when she'd first got out of the car and nodded.

'That's because nobody lives here any more,' Rob said. 'At least not in the winter. Of the twenty-two houses in the village, twelve are holiday cottages or second homes, and the prices are way beyond the reach of local youngsters. But, of course, the holidaymakers don't come here between October and March. Nobody does, except, apparently, your sister. So, why would she do that?'

Jo flushed. 'She has her reasons,' she mumbled.

'Had she come here to see someone?' Clare probed gently.

'The barman,' Jo exclaimed. The upset of finding Annabel's car had pushed the scene in the pub to the back of her mind until now.

'She came here to see Ted?' Rob's eyebrows shot up in surprise.

'No. At least I don't think so. But he recognised her, I know he did. I showed him the same photo I showed you earlier and he was just about to tell me something when Seth Carlson sent him down to the cellar. Then a few minutes later he sent his son after him.'

'Do you mean Jay?' Rob asked, wondering where this was leading to.

'A younger version of Seth. But with a bit more hair. They're so alike I assumed they were father and son.'

'Yes, that's Jay. But he wasn't in the bar when I came in.'

'No, but he had been,' Jo said. 'That's what I was trying to tell you. Seth sent him down to the cellar to coach Ted in what to say.'

Rob looked bewildered. 'I'm sorry. You've lost me. What do you mean, coach Ted? To say what?'

'It'd be laughable if it wasn't so serious,' Jo said. 'While Ted was down in the cellar, Seth spun me some nonsense about how Annabel was a dead ringer for Judy Garland and how Ted had a thing about her. Judy Garland, I mean, of course, not Annabel.'

Clare gave a hoot of laughter that made both dogs leap up and hurry across to her, their tails wagging ingratiatingly, their eyes anxious. 'The only creature Ted has ever had 'a thing about', and that included his poor late wife, I'm afraid, is his greyhound,' she said.

'No, I didn't believe it either,' Jo said. 'That's why I'm going to go back to the pub and ask Ted again.'

Rob stood up. 'If you'll take my advice — and I promise you, it's kindly meant — you'll go straight back to Wells. The chances are your sister will be back in the hotel by now and will be frantic about her car. The likeliest explanation being, of course, that it was stolen from the church car park, which regrettably does happen.'

'Yes, I'm sure you're right,' Jo

murmured, even though she was far from convinced. But, she decided, he didn't need to know that.

'Good,' he beamed. 'Now, if you'll excuse me, I must go. I've a hundred and one things to do this afternoon. Mum, thanks for lunch. It was delicious, as always.'

'I told you on the phone that I'm quite recovered now.' Clare reached up and kissed him. 'It was only a sniffle. You shouldn't have come all this way if you were so busy.'

'And miss your roast lamb? I'm never that busy. Besides, I promised Peter I'd deliver a case of port for him and check on things while he's away. Before I go,' he turned to Jo, 'let me give you my mobile number. That way, if you need me for anything, anything at all, just call me.'

They exchanged numbers and Jo stayed and finished her coffee while Clare and the dogs saw him off. As Clare returned, Jo stood up to go.

'Before you go,' Clare said, waving

aside Jo's attempt to thank her, 'I'd love to see the photo you showed Ted.'

'Yes, sure.' Jo handed it to her.

Clare looked down at the photo then took it across to the window where the light was better. 'Oh, my Lord. This is your sister?'

Jo nodded. 'So, do you think she looks like Judy Garland?'

'Oh no, my dear, not Judy Garland. But someone much closer to home.'

Jo's throat contracted. 'Somebody from Neston Parva?' she asked, her voice unnaturally tight. 'Who?'

It had to be. Jo held her breath as she waited to find out the name of the person Annabel had come to Somerset to meet.

6

Lady Eveline Staverton's violet eyes shimmered with tears. 'I realise this is a terrible thing I ask, Jacob,' she said. 'One that no one should ask of any man. But I don't ask it for myself. Nor even for my husband.' She lowered her eyes and her slender white hands twisted in her lap. 'I am with child,' she whispered. 'I ask it for the sake of my unborn baby.'

Jacob had loved Lady Eveline, from a distance of course, for as long as he'd known her. But he'd loved her husband, Roger, all his life. Loved him as a brother, for that indeed was what they were. The two half-brothers had grown up together, one the son of the Lady of the Manor, the other the son of a servant.

And if people in the village noticed how alike the two young men were, nobody commented. And certainly not to strangers. They looked after their own in Neston Parva. It had always been so.

Clare Carlson looked up from the photograph she'd been studying. 'Yes. The resemblance is uncanny. Your sister's the spitting image of a girl I went to school with. Of course, she doesn't look like that now, but . . . '

Jo's heart leapt. Ted had talked about Annabel being a dead ringer. And now Clare was talking about a spitting image. But of whom? 'Does the girl — the woman still live in Neston Parva?'

'Caroline Chalmers? Yes she does, as it happens. Only, of course, she's not Caroline Chalmers any more.'

'Don't tell me,' Jo said. 'She's another Carlson, isn't she?'

'Oh no. She did much better for herself than that.' Clare laughed. 'She's Lady Caroline now. She married Sir Peter Staverton.'

'Caroline Staverton?' Jo reached in her bag and took out the book Rob had given her. 'The woman who wrote this?'

'She did indeed. Have you read it?'

'Not all of it. But Rob told me a bit of Jacob's story, how he was hung by Judge Jeffries for his part in the Monmouth Rebellion. Was that right?'

'Certainly Jacob Carlson was hung for a rebel but whether he was one, or whether he was covering up for Sir Roger Staverton, we'll probably never know for sure.'

'The plaque on the green said something about Jacob going to his death rather than betray his friend.'

Clare shrugged. 'Well, that's Caroline's version, although I must warn you to take a lot of what she says with a large pinch of salt. As children, the pair of us were fascinated with the story of Jacob and Sir Roger. We thought it was so brave and tragic and, to be honest, after all this time I'm not even sure which bits were true and which we made up.'

'Tell me anyway,' Jo urged her, intrigued.

'In our version, Sir Roger was just twenty-one when he ran off to join Monmouth's Rebels. But when Judge Jeffries rounded them up after the defeat at Sedgemoor, everyone in Neston Parva closed ranks and swore he'd never left the village.'

'And Jacob Carlson? What happened to him?'

Clare made a face. 'He stepped forward and said it was he, and not Roger, who'd joined the Rebels. He was executed in Sir Roger's place. Lady Eveline, Sir Roger's wife, was pregnant and she was in on it, too. She may even have persuaded Jacob to do it. Of course, Sir Roger would never knowingly have stood by and let his friend hang in his place, but Lady Eveline kept him drugged and hidden away in an attic room for three weeks. By the time he came round, it was all over. And, they say, Sir Roger never forgave his wife for letting his friend go to the gallows in his place.'

'What a terrible story,' Jo said with a shudder.

Clare laughed softly. 'Terrible indeed, but only if it's true. Oh, we used to have such fun when we were children, you know, re-enacting that old story. The number of times we plagued poor Peter Staverton to let us go up in to the attic room — it has a secret staircase, you know — to see where the handsome Sir Roger lay unconscious and unknowing while his lifelong friend was executed. What bloodthirsty little girls we must have been!'

'But, assuming there's some truth in the old story, why would Jacob have done such a thing? It doesn't make sense.'

'One theory is that the two men were actually half-brothers — Jacob on the wrong side of the blanket. Certainly it's a fact that they were remarkably alike. According to Caroline's book, Jacob was in love with Lady Eveline and she persuaded him to do it to save the father of her unborn child.'

'Hence the title — *Greater Love Hath No Man*,' Jo said. 'Do you think that's what happened?'

Clare shrugged. 'As I said, who knows? But it's certainly true that Jacob Carlson was hung from the Great Neston Oak that used to stand in the middle of the village and his body was left there as a dreadful warning to all.'

Jo shivered. 'Powerful stuff,' she said.

'Yes, but I'm sure most of it is pure Caroline. She's always been the same — never happier than when she's creating some sort of drama.'

'And you say my sister looks like her?' Jo said, thinking that Annabel too had a certain flair for the dramatic.

Clare handed Jo the photo back. 'It's a remarkable likeness. And is it Caroline your sister's come to see? If so, then I'm sorry to say she's had a wasted journey. Caroline and Peter are away. They left yesterday to stay in their flat in London for a week or so.'

Now Jo understood the undercurrents, the scarcely veiled hostility in the pub. There had obviously been Carlsons and Stavertons in Neston Parva for ever, their histories inextricably linked across the centuries. Were the Carlsons, including, of course, Clare, still covering for the Stavertons? Were the Stavertons really in London? Or still here in Neston Parva?

'My dear, are you all right?' Clare asked. 'You've gone quite pale. Why not sit back for a while and have another coffee? There's plenty here.'

As Clare spoke, Rocky, the larger Dalmatian, laid his head in Jo's lap and sighed. Jo glanced down at him, fondled his silken ears then smiled as she looked up to see Clare wearing the same anxious expression as her dog.

'No thanks. I'm fine, thank you.' Jo felt more than a little guilty for having suspected Clare of being part of a conspiracy. Annabel was usually the one who saw drama and intrigue everywhere, not her.

For a moment Jo was tempted to sit back in the comfortable chair and enjoy being fussed over, if only for a little longer. But her concern for Annabel, that persistent nagging feeling that something was wrong, wouldn't allow it. She stood up, her fingers plucking at the strap of her shoulder bag. 'I'm sorry but I really must go. There's something I have to do.'

'But there's no rush, surely? You're probably still suffering from the shock of finding your sister's car like that. That was a ghastly experience.'

'Yes. Yes, it was, but I'm okay now, thanks to you and your son. But I've got to go because — ' Jo stopped herself just in time.

She'd been about to blurt out that it was because she'd just found out that Caroline Staverton must be Annabel's birth mother. It was obvious, now she thought of it. The likeness between Annabel and Caroline had been noticed by both Ted and Clare, and, presumably, Seth, all of whom would have known Caroline when she was Annabel's age.

As if to reinforce this, she remembered how, this morning back in the hotel over their coffee and croissants, when Rob had laughingly told her of Caroline's love of the dramatic and her way with words, Jo had immediately thought of Annabel, her over-active imagination and her way of dramatising everything. Was that where her flair had come from? From her birth mother? It all made perfect sense now.

'So you're going back to Wells, are you?' Clare's pleasant voice broke into Jo's racing thoughts. 'Well, I'm sure it's for the best.'

Best for whom? Why was everyone, even the pleasant and sociable Clare Carlson, so keen on getting her to leave Neston Parva? It certainly seemed to be the case that the Carlsons — and the village — appeared to be full of them. Were they still protecting the Stavertons?

But protecting them from what? Jo's

restless fingers worried at the silk scarf that hung around her neck in the same way her thoughts worried away at her peace of mind. What harm could she and Annabel do the Stavertons?

The answer almost took her breath away. What if Lady Caroline, for reasons of her own, had never told her husband about the pregnancy? In which case, Annabel's sudden appearance could, indeed, cause the Stavertons very real harm.

Oh Annabel, what have you done? Jo thought to herself. *What sort of hornet's nest have you stirred up?*

Was Jo's earlier feeling of foreboding right? Was Annabel in danger? Had she, too, fallen foul of Seth Carlson? Certainly her feisty sister would have been better at standing up to him than Jo had been. But — Jo's heart skipped a beat — suppose Annabel had been too good at standing up to him? Suppose she'd said something to anger him?

'Where does Seth Carlson live?' she asked Clare.

'Seth?' Clare looked blankly at her for a second. 'He's got a farm on the other side of the village. Of course, like so many others, he doesn't farm it much now, apart from a few beef cattle. His dairy herd is long gone. But why do you ask?'

Jo shrugged and tried to look and sound unconcerned. 'I'd like another word with him, that's all. I just had this feeling he knew more about Annabel than he let on.'

'You're not thinking of going out to the farm now, are you?' Clare asked her anxiously.

'Why not?'

'Because it's dangerous.' Clare bit her bottom lip. 'I'd really rather — '

'Dangerous?' Jo's head jerked up. 'As in shot guns . . . that sort of thing?'

'Good gracious, of course not.' Clare looked surprised. 'Whatever gave you that idea?'

'Nothing. I was just being silly.' Jo swallowed, embarrassed by her sudden outburst. 'Please go on. Dangerous in what way?'

'Seth and Jay run an Agricultural Contractors' business and keep quite a lot of valuable machinery at the farm. So they have a couple of seriously unfriendly German Shepherd guard dogs running loose. They're okay if Seth's around but if he's not . . . '

Clare bent down and stroked her dogs, that were sat, like a pair of bookends, on either side of her. 'I won't let my two anywhere near the place. And I'd hate to think of you coming up against them.'

'Me too,' Jo said with fervour. 'Thank you for the warning. My fondness for dogs extends only to the black and white spotty variety. So I think I'll take your advice and head back into Wells.'

Only, of course, she didn't. Instead, she did what she'd intended doing all along. She headed for Neston Manor, if only to prove to herself that Clare had been right when she'd said the Stavertons were away from home.

* * *

The imposing wrought iron gates swung back smoothly on well oiled hinges as Jo pushed them open. She walked up the crisp, weed-free gravel drive and paused to look up at the house before approaching the front door. It was a rambling, grey stone building with a variety of roof levels and chimney pot styles suggesting the house had been added to several times over the centuries.

Jo liked Clare Carlson and, even though it brought her no closer to finding Annabel, she was relieved to discover that it looked as if Clare had been telling the truth and that the Stavertons were indeed away. The place had that silent, watchful air of a house that has been shut up. She looked carefully at each of the tall, mullioned stone windows, looking for signs of life behind them. But the only movement came from a solitary robin foraging among the cloak of ivy that covered most of the front of the house.

Nevertheless, she gave the ancient

iron knocker several sharp raps but all she could hear was the echo of her knocking as it reverberated around the empty house. She was about to leave when the crunch of footsteps on the gravel close behind her made her whirl round.

Jay Carlson stopped so abruptly he skidded, his feet sending up a spray of gravel as he did so. He was breathing heavily, as if he'd been running and looked as surprised by her presence as she was by his.

'The house isn't open to the public until June,' he said, looking at her with a sullen, hostile expression.

'Yes, I realise that,' she said. 'I haven't come to see round the house. I came here hoping to see Lady Staverton.'

'What for?' he asked abruptly.

'I think that's between her and me, don't you?' Jo said, not bothering to hide her annoyance at his tone.

'Suit yourself. But I'll tell you this for nothing. She don't care for folk turning up without an appointment.' He stuck his hands in the pockets of his mud-covered jeans and took out a packet of cigarettes. 'I told your sister that and all.'

'You've seen Annabel?' Jo's heart did a triple somersault with joy. 'When? Where?'

'Let me see now, when was it?' With deliberate, maddening slowness he took out a cigarette and lit it, watching her carefully as he inhaled deeply before answering. 'I reckon it must have been late yesterday afternoon.'

Jo, realising he was trying to wind her up, forced herself to ask in a calm, measured voice, 'If that's the case, then why didn't you say anything when I asked about her in the pub earlier?'

'You didn't ask me.' He stared defiantly at her. Then he shrugged, looked away and focussed on scuffing a line in the gravel with the toe of his muddy boot. 'Anyway, I couldn't say anything in front of Dad, could I? The job I'd been doing finished early but he don't know that. I was dog tired and he'd have only found me something else to do if I'd gone home so I thought that I'd — '

'Do you know where my sister is now?' Jo cut in.

'Yes — and no. When I saw her yesterday she wanted to know the way to the Manor. Said she wanted to see Lady C. When I asked her if she had an appointment, she said she'd spoken to her on the phone earlier. Unlike you,' he added with a frown.

Now Jo knew beyond any doubt that her guess had been the right one. Caroline Staverton was, indeed, Annabel's birth mother and it sounded as if yesterday Annabel, thinking that Jo wouldn't be coming to join her in Somerset, had decided to go and see Caroline sooner rather than later.

'Annabel came here to see Lady Staverton yesterday afternoon?' she asked, as she looked back at the house. 'But I thought the Stavertons went away yesterday?'

He scowled. 'Who told you that?'

'Clare Carlson. She said they'd gone to their flat in London for a couple of weeks.'

Jay snorted. 'Take my advice, don't believe everything that particular lady or her toffee nosed son says.' He took another long drag on his cigarette. 'They're here all right. Least ways, they were. I saw them drive off with your sister this morning.'

'The Stavertons drove off with Annabel? This morning?' Jo wanted to shake the answers out of Jay Carlson, but knew she had to remain calm. He was the first person she'd met in Neston Parva who admitted to having seen her. The first person to confirm that she had, in fact, been here. Jo couldn't afford to upset him. 'Do you know where they were going? Did Annabel look distressed?'

'How would I know where they were going? I'm not their flippin' social secretary. I haven't the faintest idea. I just look out for the place when they're away. As for your sister looking distressed, all I can tell you is that the three of them went off in Sir Peter's Jag, all looking as happy as Larry.'

Jo could have hugged him. Instead, she thanked him then turned and walked back to her car, almost light-headed with relief.

She also felt a little foolish. So much for her wild theories about what had happened to Annabel when all the time she'd met up with the Stavertons, obviously got on so well she'd stayed the night — and, indeed, why wouldn't she, rather than go back to an empty hotel room on her own? And now she'd gone off somewhere with them. Maybe to meet other members of the family? It also explained why her car was still here — or rather, why Annabel had left her car here, she corrected herself.

There was no point in her hanging around Neston Parva any longer. Annabel could be anywhere by now. She could even be back at the Black Lion. In which case, Jo ought to get back there as soon as possible so she could tell her about the car.

She got back to her own car and switched on the engine. But instead of driving off as she'd intended, she sat for a moment, her hands resting on the steering wheel, her forehead creased in a deep frown as something niggled away at her.

Something she'd been told today didn't add up. But what was it exactly? And by whom?

7

Lady Eveline looked down at the still figure of her husband, slumped across the table and turned, as she always did when she was in need of help, to Jacob.

'You must help me, Jacob,' she said. 'I cannot move him on my own.'

Jacob stepped forward and lifted the limp figure up in his arms, as gently and effortlessly as if he was lifting a child. Roger gave a small moan and Lady Eveline's hand went to her mouth.

'He's waking up, Jacob,' she gasped. 'Maybe I didn't give him a strong enough potion.'

'Not him,' Jacob said with a smile. 'He sleeps well, as he always does. Have no fear. Where do you want me to take him?'

'There's a small attic room at the top of the house. The small stairway is cleverly concealed behind what appears to be an old cupboard. He'll be safely out of the way there. No one will know he's there. And, by administering the potion to him every day, I can keep him safely out of the way while you — '

'While I take his place on the scaffold,' Jacob said quietly as he carried his friend, brother and the husband of the only woman he would ever love up the two flights of stairs to the attic-room.

'Wait,' Lady Eveline called him back. 'I cannot let you do this, Jacob. There must be another way.'

'There is no other way. You have no choice, my Lady,' he said quietly as he gently laid his friend on the narrow bed.

As Jo sat in her car, puzzling over what it was she was missing, her phone began to ring. As it did so, something clicked inside her head and she cursed herself for not having thought of it before. Annabel might travel without a toothbrush or even a change of clothes at a push but not her precious phone. Yet the last time Jo had seen it, it had been on the passenger seat of her car.

Annabel's phone, as Jo was always teasing her, was an extension of her right hand. She'd never go anywhere without it. At least not willingly. Which meant, surely, that Jay Carlson was lying.

She glared down at her persistently ringing phone. Why didn't whoever it was give up and leave her alone? If it was Matt again . . . She checked the caller ID. It wasn't Matt or any number she recognised. She was about to switch it off without answering it when it occurred to her that it could be someone with news of Annabel.

'Hello?'

'Jo? Rob Carlson. I'm glad I caught you.'

Jo's heart lurched. 'What is it? Have you heard anything? Is Annabel back at the hotel?'

'No, I'm afraid she's not. I'm not at

the hotel but I've just rung them and they say she's not come back yet.'

'I see. Well, thank you for letting me know.' It was nothing more than she'd expected but for a brief moment she'd allowed herself to hope. She was about to end the call when he spoke again.

'Wait, please, Jo. There's something I meant to ask you earlier, but we were overtaken by events.' His voice was soft, hesitant even, and so very different from the strong decisive man who'd taken control by the side of the rhine a couple of hours ago.

'What is it?' she asked.

'It's just — well, I realise you may not feel like it, what with everything that's been going on today or you have other plans but I — er — well, I wondered if you'd like to have dinner with me this evening?'

An invitation to dinner was the last thing she'd expected and she felt a warm glow spread through her.

'That's really kind of you,' she said, hating having to turn him down but having no choice. She couldn't even think of going out on a date, enjoying herself, until she'd found Annabel. 'But I'm afraid — '

'Please say yes,' he said. 'It's the very least I can do after the way a member of my staff treated you last night.'

Jo froze, thankful he couldn't see the way her cheeks reddened as she realised how close she'd come to making a fool of herself. What had she been thinking of? Did she honestly think he'd been asking her out on a date? A proper wining and dining date because he enjoyed her company? Idiot that she was, he was just doing his job, that was all. Trying to safeguard his hotel's good name. Didn't he say as much this morning when she'd first made her complaint about the young receptionist, Nikki, or whatever her name was? He'd even mentioned the word compensation.

'That won't be necessary, thank you.' Embarrassment made her voice sharper than she'd intended. 'You more than made up for that when you jumped in the rhine,' she added more gently, remembering how grateful she'd been — indeed, still was to him. 'Sorry Rob, I've got to — there's somewhere I have to go.'

'That wouldn't be Seth Carlson's place, would it?' His voice was edgy now, bristling with barely concealed irritation. 'Mum called me. She's worried you might be thinking of going there. For pity's sake, what is it with you? Why do you never take advice?'

Jo had never been particularly good at standing up for herself. All her life she'd been the one to back down. Sometimes, she'd be so anxious to keep the peace, she'd apologise, even when she wasn't the one in the wrong. But today, fuelled no doubt by her worry about Annabel, something had changed. She'd stood up to Seth Carlson — more or less — and she certainly wasn't going to let Rob Carlson tell her off.

'I resent being spoken to as if I was seven years old, Mr Carlson,' she said frostily. 'I don't have to account to anyone for my movements, least of all you.'

'No, of course not,' he said quickly. 'And now I've upset you, and I'm really, really sorry. That was the last thing I intended. Please forgive me. I shouldn't have spoken to you like that. My only excuse is that I am worried about you, as indeed, is my mother. She's not given to exaggeration, you know. Her warning about Seth's dogs was spot on.'

As Jo remembered Clare's kindness to her, her anger melted away and she felt ashamed of her snippy reaction which, she was honest enough to admit to herself, was as much to do with her still smarting from having so nearly made a fool of herself over Rob's dutiful dinner invitation. 'Of course it was,' she said in a low voice. 'And I'm sorry, too. I — I didn't mean . . . '

But her words of apology petered out as she remembered something else Clare had told her which pushed everything else from her mind.

'Look, I'm sorry. I really am. But I must go,' she said. 'And I promise you, I won't go within a mile of Seth and his dogs.'

She ended the call, her heart pounding. Annabel hadn't been driven off by the Stavertons this morning. That, of course, was just a story Jay had made up to draw her away from the Manor. And she'd almost fallen for it.

But not any more. Because now she knew where Annabel might be. It was the slenderest of leads but the only one she'd got. And it was Clare who'd given her the clue.

She was going to find her sister. But to do that, she had to go back up the long driveway to Neston Manor and once again confront Jay Carlson.

★ ★ ★

Jo stood on the gravel and once again looked up at the Manor's higher windows, one of which, she could see, had bars on it. Was that the attic room where Lady Eveline had hidden Sir Roger all those years ago? The room in which the young Caroline used to play at being Lady Eveline? The one with the secret, hidden staircase?

Annabel had been at the Manor yesterday. In that one thing, Jo was sure, Jay was telling the truth. And could that attic room also be the place where the adult Caroline, or somebody acting on her behalf, had hidden Annabel?

'Back so soon?' This time she hadn't heard Jay coming up behind her and his sudden appearance made her jump. 'You're surely not still looking for that sister of yours, are you? You don't give up, I'll say that for you.'

'I was looking for you.' Jo looked at him levelly. 'Because I don't think Annabel drove off with the Stavertons at all this morning. In fact, I think she's here in this house. Maybe in that room up there. The one with the bars on the window.'

Jay scowled. 'Are you calling me a

liar?' He took a step towards her, his voice heavy with menace.

Jo steeled herself to stand her ground. 'I think maybe you were mistaken,' she said, sounding a lot more confident than she felt. 'I think you may have seen someone else in the car with the Stavertons, but not my sister. Because I think — no, I know, my sister is in this house.'

'If you're so sure of yourself, why don't you knock on the door?' He gave a sudden grin, which was far more disturbing than his previous scowl. 'Who knows? Maybe your sister will answer it.'

'I think she's being held against her will and what's more, I'm going to call the police.' She took her phone from her bag.

'And in the meantime?'

'What do you mean?' She stared at him, uneasily. Why was he looking so smug and pleased with himself?

'I mean, what are you going to do while you're waiting the thirty, maybe forty minutes it will take them to get here?' He smirked. 'If, that is, they come at all. After all, they've already been out this way once this afternoon. It'll be at least two months before they're anywhere near here again. Haven't you heard of the sad decline in rural policing? Of course I blame the Government myself . . . '

As he was speaking, Jo's hand tightened on her phone. Jay stopped mid-sentence, a look of alarm on his face as Annabel's distinctive ringtone shrilled out. Jo couldn't work out where the sound was coming from and looked around, expecting to see Annabel standing behind her, her phone to her ear. But there was no one there.

Then she realised what had happened. She must have hit the number one key, Annabel's speed dial number, by mistake. The ringing sound was coming from Jay's pocket.

'It was you, wasn't it?' Jo rounded on him. 'You took Annabel's car, didn't you? That's why you were covered in mud just now — and you still haven't made that good a job of cleaning yourself up.' She began to back away. 'That's my sister's phone ringing in your pocket. I'd know her ringtone anywhere. You took it when you pushed her car into the rhine. Go on then, answer it. Prove to me I'm wrong.'

He looked at her, his dark eyes wary. Then he grinned and shrugged. 'And what if I did take it? It was just lying there on the front seat, asking to be stolen. It seemed a crying shame to let a good piece of kit like that go to waste,' he drawled, his usual smirk now back in place. 'And where do you think you're going?'

'Away from you — you monster. I'm going straight to the police.'

'And leave your poor little sister all alone? When she really needs you? Or let's put it this way — she needs someone, that's for sure. At least, that's what I thought the last time I saw her. A doctor? Maybe even an ambulance? But what do I know? I'm no medical expert.'

Jo stiffened as fear trailed an icy finger down her back. 'Where is she?' she whispered.

'Where do you think?'

Jo looked up at the attic window. 'Oh God, I was right all the time. She's in there, isn't she?'

'Smart girl,' he murmured. 'Got it in one. Go to the top of the class.'

'If you've hurt her . . . '

'Well now, that's something you're going to have to find out for yourself, isn't it? You coming?'

He held up a key, waved it at her and began to walk around the side of the house to a back door. Jo hurried after him. 'What do you think you're doing?' she asked as he unlocked the door.

'Taking that damn thing off you for a start,' he said menacingly, grabbing her mobile roughly.

'Give that back,' she cried but he'd already disappeared into the house. She followed him in to a large kitchen. At any other time she'd have loved the room, the sort she'd dreamt of since childhood, with its dark green Aga that gave out a gentle heat, the blue willow patterned plates that adorned an old cream-painted dresser. But she hardly gave it a glance as she hurried to catch up, following Jay along a dark, wood-panelled passage, then up a broad, elegant staircase.

'This used to be a secret staircase, you know,' Jay said as he stood at the bottom of a second flight of stairs. 'But the previous Lady Staverton had the false cupboard taken away when my dad locked the present Sir Peter in there and went home without telling anyone. It took them several hours to find him.'

Still chuckling to himself, he went up the narrow flight of stairs, where every other tread creaked and squeaked. They reached a dark, windowless landing and he pointed to a closed door straight ahead which Jo could just make out in the dim light.

'Annabel's in there?' Jo forgot all about getting her phone back from Jay as she stood in front of the door, sick with apprehension.

There was a bolt on the top of the door. He slid it across and slowly pushed the door open. Jo took a few steps forward so that she could see beyond him in to the room.

The light wasn't very good but there was enough for her to make out a narrow, iron-framed bed. And on it, lay a figure, one arm trailed over the side, her long hair spread across the pillow like rich, brown silk.

It was Annabel. And she wasn't moving.

8

'Annabel?' Jo whispered and moved towards her. She hardly noticed when Jay closed the door behind her and slid the bolt across. Hardly cared that he had just shut them both in the small attic room or that she had walked into his trap.

The only thing she cared about was the fact that Annabel lay on the bed without moving. Without, it seemed, breathing.

'Bel? Can you hear me?' She picked up Annabel's limp wrist, relieved beyond measure when she felt the steady rhythm of a pulse beneath her fingers. 'It's Jo. Come on, wake up. Time to get up now.' She shook her sister's shoulder gently and Annabel's answering groan was the sweetest sound she'd ever heard.

She ran to the door and thumped it

with her fist. 'Jay?' she yelled. 'Can you hear me? Go and get a doctor, please. She's sick. Annabel's sick. Please, Jay.'

'It's Jacob.' His voice sounded so close he had to be standing on the other side of the door. 'My name is Jacob. And don't worry about your sister. She doesn't need to see a doctor. She'll be fine when the sedative wears off.'

'Sedative? What have you given her, you madman?'

There was silence.

'Jay? Are you still there?' She fought to keep the panic out of her voice. 'Please, please don't leave us. Annabel needs help.'

'I told you, my name is Jacob,' he said. 'I don't like being called Jay and I'm no madman.'

Jo could have called him a lot worse than that, but she bit it back. It was not a good idea to antagonise him. 'Okay, okay, I'm sorry . . . Jacob.' Her breath came in panicky little gasps. 'I'm sorry. But . . . but I don't understand. Why are you doing this? What do you want from us? Is it money? We're not rich, but we — '

'I don't want your money.' He sounded almost offended.

'Then what is it? I don't get it.' She leaned her face against the door and fought against the panic that was threatening to overwhelm her. 'Please, Jacob, just tell me what you want. Please.'

'I'll tell you what I want. I want you and your precious sister to go away and never come back. Forget you've ever been here. Forget everything. No interviews, no story. Nothing.'

'I promise you, word of honour, we'll leave Neston Parva, leave Somerset in fact and never, ever, come back. I promise.' It was the easiest promise she'd ever made. If — no, she corrected herself hastily, when she and Annabel got out of this damn room, nothing on earth would persuade her to come back to this hell-hole. Ever.

'No story?'

Jo had no idea what he meant but she

was so anxious to get Annabel to a doctor and she'd have promised him anything. 'No story. I promise you'll never hear from us again. And — and I promise, if you let us go, I won't tell a living soul about this. Now, will you open the door, Jacob? Please.'

Even without seeing his face, she could sense his indecision. 'But what about her?' he asked. 'How can I be sure?'

'Look, Jacob. Kidnapping, unlawful imprisonment, whatever you call it, is a very serious crime. You could go to jail for a long time. Surely you don't want that?'

'It wouldn't be the first time a Carlson sacrificed his liberty for a Staverton.' Jay's voice rang with pride.

Jo caught her breath. Was that what this was all about? He saw himself as the reincarnation of Jacob Carlson? Protecting the Staverton's honour? But from what?

'My sister has no intention of harming the Stavertons, Jacob,' she said earnestly, desperate to make him understand. 'You must believe that.'

'Sir Peter's not a well man. He's gone up to London for some big heart op. Lady C's worried sick about him, that's the truth. Nikki and me, we heard her telling my dad the other night. They didn't know we were listening and we also heard her tell Dad that your sister's a journalist. She told Dad he had to do something about it, that it was time he took some responsibility. Well, he's all mouth and trousers is my dad. I knew he wasn't going to do anything to stop her, but I did. While he was standing around, dithering, I just got on and did it.'

'But, Jacob, listen to me. Annabel means them no harm,' she repeated, hoping that if she said it often enough, he'd have to believe her.

'Means them no harm? That's what she says, but journalists are all the same. They let you think they're okay, that they're your friend, then they trick you in to saying things you don't mean. And when they get back to their papers, they write lies. I've seen it for myself. I can't let that happen again.'

'Jay — sorry, Jacob. Listen to me. Annabel is a journalist, yes. But that's not why she's here.' She took a deep breath and prayed she was doing the right thing. But she had to convince him and could think of no other way. 'She's here because she's recently found out that Caroline Staverton is her birth mother.'

The silence on the other side of the door was so complete, Jo began to think he'd crept silently away. 'Jacob? Answer me. Jacob, are you there?'

'I'm still here,' he growled angrily, 'and I don't believe you. That is a filthy lie. I was right all along, wasn't I? She's just like the rest of them. Means them no harm? Course she does. She has even invented this sick lie about Lady C which she'll no doubt sell to the highest bidder. When the story gets out, this place will be swarming with the press. They'll be crawling all over us like maggots.'

She heard his footsteps on the stairs. 'Please. Please don't leave us,' she cried. 'At least get Annabel some water. Please.'

But there was no answer. Just the sound of his heavy footsteps, and the creak of every other tread, getting fainter and fainter until they disappeared altogether.

Then nothing. Nothing but a deep, empty silence, broken only by the pure, liquid notes of a robin singing outside the window.

'Jay. Come back,' she yelled. 'You can't leave us here like this.'

She threw herself at the door and cried out as her shoulder crunched against the all too solid oak. She gave the handle one last despairing shake, then put her ear to the door, straining to hear the creak of his returning footsteps on the stairs.

'Jo? What's wrong?' Annabel's voice was little more than a hoarse whisper, but it was the best sound in the world to Jo.

She whirled round, staring at her sister while her muscles turned to water and her eyes stung with a rush of sudden, hot tears.

'You're awake. Thank God.' She rushed across to the bed and helped Annabel to sit up, putting the thin pillow at her back. 'Boy, did you give me a scare. For a minute back there, I thought . . . Are you all right?'

'I've been better.' Annabel rubbed her temples, her eyes unfocussed, her face ashen. 'My head feels like it's full of cotton wool. My mouth, too.' She frowned at her watch, shook it then peered at it again. 'What's the time? My watch must have stopped.'

'Half past three.'

Annabel shook her head. 'It can't be.'

'Do you remember how you got here?' Jo asked gently, not wanting to alarm Annabel but needing to know how much she remembered.

For the first time Annabel looked around the dim room. 'God, yes. I'm at Neston Manor, aren't I? What are you doing here anyway?' Her eyes were clearer now as she turned to Jo. 'I thought you had plans for the weekend?'

'I'll tell you later,' Jo said. 'Go on, you were saying you came to Neston Manor. Why?'

'When you said you wouldn't come with me, I drove out here to see what the place looked like. Just curious, that's all. But then this chap turned up and asked me what I was doing.'

'That would be Jay Carlson.'

'He didn't say what his name was. But he seemed to think I'd come here to interview Caroline Staverton and I went along with it because he said he'd take me to her.' She massaged her temples. 'Have you got any aspirin in that suitcase you insist on calling a handbag? My head's bursting.'

'I'm sorry. I've got some chocolate, though, if that will help.' She gave the bar to Annabel. 'Are you able to go on? You were saying how you came here yesterday and — '

'Not yesterday. This afternoon.'

'But, Bel,' Jo said gently, 'today's Saturday. You came here yesterday. Friday afternoon.'

'Yesterday? That's not possible.' At the sight of Annabel's bewildered face Jo could have cheerfully strangled Jay Carlson if he'd been within range. 'My head's so muzzy,' she leaned back against the pillow. 'Help me, Jo. I can't think straight. Tell me what I'm doing here. I — I don't remember.'

'Don't worry.' Jo laid a soothing hand on her sister's clammy forehead. 'It'll come back. I think Jay Carlson said he'd take you to Caroline. He brought you up here — '

'Yes. Yes. That's it. It's coming back now. He was actually very nice, gave me a coffee, showed me up here to what he called a very special room, one that meant an awful lot to her but that she'd explain it all. Then he said he'd go and hurry her up. Yes, it's all coming back now. I finished my coffee then sat down for a while, wondering what to do next.

137

Then I thought I'd go and see if anyone was about. I — I thought they'd forgotten about me, you see. But the door jammed. I couldn't open it. And then . . . ' she shook her head. 'You see, that's the bit I still can't get my head around. After that, nothing. The next thing I know, you're banging on the door, screaming like a banshee. What's going on?'

'You've been drugged. It must have been in the coffee.'

Annabel stared at her and let the piece of chocolate she'd been about to put in her mouth fall from her fingers. Her face was the colour of putty. 'Is this a wind up?'

'I wish it was.' Jo took Annabel's hand in her own. 'Look, I don't want to frighten you but you've got to know. We're both locked in here now.'

'By this Jay person?' Annabel's nails dug in to Jo's palm as her grasp tightened. 'Why? What does he want?'

'I wish I knew,' Jo sighed. 'He's a complete odd ball. He thinks he's the reincarnation of some chap from a tale of seventeenth-century heroics when his family protected the Stavertons. Jacob Carlson went to the gallows in place of Sir Roger Staverton. At least that's the version in Caroline's book. Although the truth is probably quite different.'

'Caroline's a writer?' Jo was pleased to see some colour return to Annabel's cheeks. 'Well, what do you know? That must be where I get it from, Jo.'

'I don't know about her being a writer. I've been told she only wrote the book to attract visitors to the Manor. Anyway, Jay said he'd overheard Caroline and his father fretting about you being a journalist. Although why that should bother them, I've no idea.'

'Ah right. I think I have. Jo, don't you know who Sir Peter Staverton is?'

'Should I?'

'You would if you kept up-to-date with current affairs. He's the ex-MP who chaired a corruption enquiry a few years back, the man the tabloids tried hard to discredit. One of them even ran a story about him being involved in crooked land deals which turned out to be a complete lie. There was a huge fuss about it, questions in the House, all that sort of thing. Surely you remember?'

'Of course I do. It was hard to miss. But — ' Jo looked at her sister with increasing concern. 'Are you all right? You've gone very pale all of a sudden. Perhaps you'd better lie down again.'

'No. I'm fine. Well, actually, I'm not fine because I've just realised . . . Caroline — she — all that talk on the phone. She never meant it, did she? About how she was looking forward to seeing me? She probably wasn't even here. It was a mobile number I called, after all. She set me up, Jo. My own mother set me up. And in doing so she's put us both in danger. I'm so sorry. If only I hadn't — '

'Don't,' Jo said firmly as Annabel's voice choked with tears. 'You don't know Caroline was involved. After all, according to what you told me she wasn't really expecting you yesterday, was she? That was Jay's version of events, remember? And he's not — Ssh. Listen.'

'What is it? What do you hear?' Annabel whispered, alerted by the urgency in her sister's voice.

'Jay's coming back.'

From the other side of the door came the sound of footsteps on creaking floorboards getting closer and closer.

'Stay there,' Jo hissed to Annabel as she went across to a bookcase on the other side of the room. She emptied her shoulder bag, sending a golden shower of beads from the broken necklace raining on to the floor as she did so. Then she crammed as many heavy books as she could fit into her now empty bag.

'What on earth . . . ' Annabel began but Jo motioned her to silence as the footsteps drew closer. She crept behind the door, the arm holding the bag drawn back to shoulder height.

There was a teeth jarring screech as

141

the bolt was pulled back. The door opened and he stepped into the room. Jo came up behind him, swung the weighted bag as hard as she could and caught him squarely between the shoulders. The force of the blow sent shock waves up her arm.

As she did so, Annabel screamed, 'No, Jo. Don't!'

Her warning came too late.

He gave a grunt, part surprise, part pain and staggered forward. He'd almost recovered his balance when he slid on the loose beads. With flailing arms, he crashed to the floor, pulling over a rickety cane table as he did so. The coffee cup that had been on the table shattered, sending shards of blue pottery skittering across the wooden floor to lie among the golden beads.

'What have you done?' Annabel scrabbled off the bed and went across to the prone figure. 'He's not moving.'

'What have I done?' Jo's struggled for breath. 'This is the man who kidnapped us and drugged you. I used reasonable force. Isn't that what they say?'

'But he isn't. That's what I was trying to tell you. This isn't Jay Carlson.'

Jo's bag slipped from her fingers.

'Not Jay?' she whispered, her heart thudding. 'Then who?'

9

As Roger Staverton struggled to open his eyes, the first person he saw was his wife, her face drawn and pale, her eyes heavy with anxiety as she looked down at him.

'What happened?' he said, easing himself up into a sitting position, alarmed at how weak and faint he felt. 'Have I been ill?'

'Yes,' she said. 'But you are well now.'

'What was wrong with me?' He rubbed his head then looked around him. 'And what am I doing in here? Why am I not in my own bedchamber? Help me out because, in truth, I feel as weak as a newborn lamb.'

'I cannot,' she said. 'My condition . . . '

'No, of course not. I'm sorry. I forgot. My head — it feels like a canon is pounding away inside it. Go and ask

Jacob to come and help me.'

Her eyes filled with tears. 'Roger, my darling husband, there's something you should know . . . '

Jo knelt beside the still figure of the man she'd just felled. She touched his shoulder and as she did so, Rob Carlson opened his eyes. So bright, so blue and so gloriously, thankfully alive — if a little confused.

'What happened?' He pulled himself into a sitting position and looked around the room. 'Jo?' He frowned as he tried to make sense of the situation. 'What are you doing here? And what the hell hit me?'

'I'm afraid I did.' Jo helped him up.

'You did? But why?'

'I didn't mean to — or rather I did mean to, but not to you. Here, sit on the bed for a minute. Are you all right?'

He ran his fingers gingerly across the back of his head and winced. 'I've got a lump the size of an egg,' he said, 'but I'll survive. I've got a pretty tough skull.

What did you hit me with?'

Jo indicated her bag. 'With that,' she said. 'I'm so sorry. I thought you were Jay.'

'Jay? What's he — ?' He stopped, his frown replaced by a look of incredulity. 'The bolt. It was across the door, wasn't it? Are you telling me Jay locked you in here?'

'Got it in one. When I heard the door open, I thought it was him coming back, so I weighted my bag with books, hid behind the door and whacked him as hard as I could.' Her voice faltered. 'Only it wasn't him. It was you. I'm really, really sorry. Are you sure you're all right?'

'I'll live.' He turned to Annabel. 'And you, I take it, are Jo's sister?'

'I'm Annabel — and are we glad to see you, even if my sister has an odd way of showing it! According to her, I've been locked in here since yesterday afternoon, but I still can't believe it.'

'How did you know we were here?' Jo asked.

'I didn't,' he said. 'I was looking for Jay. Seth didn't know where he was but thought he might be up here, doing some work in the grounds. I had to come here anyway to deliver Peter's case of port. As I got here, I saw Jay, not in the grounds where I'd expected to find him but coming down the stairs. He spun some story about doing a job in the attic for Caroline.'

Jo heard Annabel's intake of breath and squeezed her hand.

'You didn't believe him?' Jo asked.

'I've known my cousin all my life and can usually tell when he's up to something. So I thought I'd take a look around, just in case. Then I saw the door to this room was closed, which is unusual as Caroline's cat loves to sleep up here on the window sill. I came up to check she hadn't been shut in by mistake.'

'Instead of which, you found us,' Jo said with a shiver.

'You're saying Jay did this deliber-ately?' Rob asked. 'That doesn't make sense. I know he can be an idiot, but — '

'Sense or not, that's exactly what he did,' Jo said, 'and what's more, he drugged my sister. Look, do you think we could get out of here? Annabel and I have seen more than enough of this horrible little room.'

'Of course. Let's go.' Rob looked so genuinely shocked that any lingering doubts Jo may have had about his involvement in Annabel's kidnap disappeared. 'Do you need any help?' he asked Annabel as she stood up unsteadily.

'No, I'm fine, thanks.'

'Is there a Police Station in Wells?' Jo asked.

'I'll take you there straight away.'

'Do you mind taking us to the hotel first?' Annabel said. 'I need a shower and change of clothes before I do anything else. I'm not feeling at my best.'

'Do you think that's wise?' Jo said. 'Every minute we delay, we're giving Jay and Seth even more time to put their story together. Or even make a bolt for it.'

'Seth?' Rob stared at her. 'You surely don't think Seth had anything to do with this, do you?'

'Of course. In the pub, just minutes before you came in, he threatened me.' Even now, the memory of Seth's menacing look made her heart thud. Was he as mad as his son? 'He thinks he's the reincarnation of Jacob Carlson, you know.'

'Seth does?' He laughed. 'Now I know you're not serious.'

'I mean Jay. He told me to call him Jacob and kept banging on about how the Carlsons always looked out for the Stavertons.' She took the books out of her bag and scooped the small pile of her belongings, minus the beads, back into it.

'I think you forgot this.' Rob bent down and picked up the bright pink fluffy mouse. 'Caroline's cat has enough of the real thing to keep her busy.'

Jo's cheeks reddened as she took the mouse and stuffed it back in her bag. 'It's not for me,' she muttered.

'I'm glad to hear it,' he said with a smile.

For a second, Jo was tempted to snap that this was no laughing matter. But then she felt something inside her give way. It was, she realised, the hard knot of anger that had enabled her to get through this whole nightmare. But now it was over. She didn't need it any more. Tentatively, she smiled back as the nightmare began to recede.

Rob was brilliant. He took them to the Black Lion, sorted out a room for Jo next to Annabel's, the room she should have had originally, before Nikki intervened. He also organised for her luggage to be collected and brought across from the Crown.

'You go and have your shower. I'll send up a tray of tea and sandwiches,' he told them. 'Take as long as you need. I promise you, Jay Carlson is not going anywhere. I'll see to that.'

Jo had just got into her room and was about to close the door when she heard Annabel say, 'Can I help you?'

There was a tinge of uncertainty in her voice that sent alarm bells ringing in Jo's head. She ran to Annabel's room and pushed open the door. Seth Carlson stood facing Annabel, a grim expression on his dark face.

'Get out before I call the police,' Jo said as she reached for the phone.

'No, wait,' Annabel said. 'He says he's got a message from Caroline.'

'The last time a member of your family had a message from Caroline, Annabel was kidnapped.' Jo glared intently at Seth. 'Your son is going to jail for this.'

'They can lock the idiot up and throw away the key,' he growled. 'I've not come to plead mercy for him.'

'Then what have you come for?' Jo asked.

'To put things right. Or as right as they can be.' He turned to Annabel. 'You wrote to Caroline, saying you'd like to meet her, right?'

Annabel nodded. 'Then we spoke on the phone and she said to come down. That's why I came here. Where is she?'

'She's not here just now. Her husband's got a serious heart condition. They've gone down to London for him to have by-pass surgery.'

'But I only spoke to Caroline a couple of days ago,' Annabel said.

'You know how these things happen. The hospital phoned to say they'd had a cancellation and that was that. Off they went. They'd been on standby for a couple of weeks.'

'You mean Caroline didn't know about this — she didn't get Jay to — ?' Jo could hear the relief in Annabel's voice. 'In that case, I don't understand?'

'Rob told me what happened to you. It appears Jay and his girlfriend overheard me and Caroline talking about you. Being Jay he got hold of the wrong end of the stick. He heard us say that you were a journalist and he thought that was why we were so upset.

Peter had a bad time with the tabloids a few years back and Jay wanted to protect him.'

'The Carlsons protecting the Stavertons,' Jo murmured. 'You know he prefers to be called Jacob, not Jay?'

Seth swore softly. 'I blame Caroline for that,' he muttered. 'She fills his head with nonsense then leaves me to sort out the mess.'

'And is that what I am?' Annabel asked, her eyes glittering. 'Am I just part of the mess?'

Seth's face softened. He made a movement towards her, as if to offer comfort, then pulled back, his large hands hanging by his side. 'Of course not,' he said awkwardly.

'But I didn't mean them any harm,' Annabel said. 'My reasons for wanting to meet her had nothing to do with her husband. Or me being a journalist. It was . . . ' she paused, 'personal.'

'You're her daughter,' Seth said.

'She told you?' Annabel's eyes widened.

'Not at the time, no.' There was a strange, almost wistful expression on his face. 'If she had, who knows how things might have turned out?'

'Sorry? I don't understand,' Annabel said. But Jo did. She understood only too well where the conversation was leading and wondered why Annabel couldn't see it.

Seth walked across the room to the window and stared out.

'We were just a couple of kids. You know how it is. We'd been going out together for a couple of months, nothing serious, just boy and girl stuff. But this particular night we both had a bit too much to drink and . . . ' He paused and raked his hands through his hair. 'Well, I suppose you'd say we got carried away. I didn't even know she was pregnant. In fact, I didn't see her after that night, not for years. She was whipped off to London to stay with an aunt and I was told she'd gone there to work and wouldn't be back. No phone calls, no letters, nothing. When she did come back a few years later, she took up with Peter and that was that.'

Jo watched Annabel while Seth was speaking and saw the jolt of shock as the truth sank in at last. Jo opened the mini-bar and poured out a large measure of brandy, worried by her sister's increasingly pale face.

'Are you okay?' Jo asked quietly as she handed the drink to Annabel.

Annabel nodded, her face ashen, her eyes huge. 'Go on,' she said to Seth in a small, quiet voice.

'When you got in touch with her, out of the blue like that, she panicked,' he said. 'Called me in quite a state. She didn't know what to do. We talked about it and, in the end, she asked me to see you on her behalf and tell you the whole story. She made me swear that I'd get you to promise never to tell a soul before I said a word. But I reckon you're entitled to the truth. So I'll tell you and leave it up to you what you do. Between us, we've all done you enough harm. It's time for the truth, whatever the consequences.'

'So what is it?' Annabel asked.

Seth shifted in his chair.

'The thing is — Peter and Caroline . . . well, they never had any children. It just didn't happen. It didn't bother her. Not the maternal type, she says. But it bothered her that it bothered him, if you see what I mean.'

Annabel nodded. 'I suppose he wanted someone to carry on the Staverton line.'

'No, he didn't care about that so much. But Peter's a pretty old-fashioned sort of chap. If he thought their failure to have children was down to him, he'd take it very hard. It would make him feel less of a man, according to Caroline.'

'But that's nonsense,' Annabel said.

Seth gave a wry smile. 'That's Peter for you. Anyway, Caroline never told him about the baby — about you, I mean. It's something she's always felt guilty about. So, as much to make up for that as anything else, she told him she'd had the test and it showed that it was her fault, not his.'

'But surely — '

'You're living proof that wasn't true,' Seth finished the sentence for her. 'And that was her problem when you turned up out of the blue like that, asking to see her. Shook her rigid, it did. She's worried sick about Peter at the moment, with him being so ill and waiting for this op, that she's not really thinking straight. All she knows is she doesn't want anything to upset him at the moment. She says she promises she will tell him about you, when he's a little stronger.'

Annabel sipped the brandy and Jo was relieved to see some of the colour return. 'But I still don't see why Jay kidnapped me. Unless . . . ' She put the glass down quickly. 'You don't think he was going to kill me, do you?'

'Kill you?' Seth laughed. 'That boy couldn't harm a fly.'

'Well, he certainly tried to harm Annabel,' Jo flashed. 'So you'll excuse us if we don't share your amusement.'

Before she could say any more there was a tap at the door and a waitress came in, carrying a tray.

'Mr Carlson said you might like this,' she said, putting the tray down on the table. Then she straightened up and turned to Annabel, her expression a mixture of fear and defiance. 'He also said you'd want to speak to me.'

Annabel looked puzzled. But Jo knew exactly who she was — and why she'd been sent up here. And it had very little to do with afternoon tea.

'You're the girl who was on duty last night, aren't you?' Jo said. 'The girl who said Annabel wasn't in the hotel and sent me on a wild goose chase. Why did you do that?'

Nikki flushed and looked at Seth. 'It's a bit — well, I'd rather not say anything in front of him, if you don't mind.'

'Well, I mind,' Seth growled.

'I don't think it's up to you,' Jo said sharply to him. 'Unless, of course, there's anything else you have to tell us?'

'Yes, there damn well is.' Seth stood up and glared at Nikki. 'Starting with Little Miss Butter Wouldn't Melt in Her Mouth here. You do know who she is, don't you?'

Annabel shook her head. Nikki looked down at the floor.

'She's my son's girlfriend, that's who she is. And if I know anything about it, she's the one who put him up to all this nonsense. The whole sorry mess has got her name written all over it.'

'Sit down, Seth,' Annabel said. 'Whatever Nikki's got to say, she can say it in front of you.' She turned to Jo. 'What's all this about?'

'When I first spoke to Nikki on the phone yesterday,' Jo explained, 'she told me you were staying at this hotel and booked me a room next to yours. The one I'm in now, I should imagine. Yet when I arrived an hour later, she said you weren't here and that I must have phoned the wrong hotel. I was so tired after my journey that, for the moment, I believed her and went instead to the Crown.' She turned to Nikki.

Nikki flushed. 'It wasn't me you spoke to that first time.'

'Of course it was,' Jo said.

'No, you spoke to one of the waitresses who was covering for me.' She looked down at her hands. 'I'd slipped out for a while to meet Jay. If Rob — Mr Carlson — found out what I'd done, I'd be in trouble.'

'Like you're not already?' Jo said sharply, as tears filled the girl's panda-like eyes.

She nodded. 'He says if I keep my job, which he's still thinking about, I'll be back to waitressing again, which is so not fair because — '

'It sounds more than fair to me,' Jo said grimly. 'So, come on, you still haven't explained why you lied to me.'

'When I saw your name in the reservation book and realised you were another Miss Frankley, it gave me a real fright. I'd already had to speak to Jay about your sister.' She turned round to

Annabel now. 'About you going out to visit Neston Manor. You came down and asked me directions on how to get there.'

'Of course,' Annabel said. 'I remember now. You were the girl on the reception with the long silver earrings.'

Nikki nodded.

'I knew then that you were going to try and see Caroline and sent Jay out there to head you off. Then, when your sister turned up, well, I just told him to make sure he kept you away from each other. That was all. We never meant either of you any harm.'

This time it was Seth who spoke. 'I don't get this,' he said, looking puzzled. 'That son of mine is daft, but he's not a criminal. Just criminally stupid. How the hell did you get him to do something as serious as kidnapping someone?'

Nikki flushed. 'I knew she was a journalist,' she said. 'And you know how Jay has this thing about journalists. I just wound him up a bit about it. Told him it was happening all over again.'

Seth swore again. 'Aye, that would do it. You see, a few years ago there was a lot of bother with journalists. Peter — '

'Was falsely accused of corruption,' Annabel finished his sentence. 'Yes, I remember. I was telling Jo about it this afternoon.'

'Well, one of these so called gentlemen of the press tricked Jay into telling him more than he should have about Peter. The poor lad was horrified when he saw how his words had been twisted the next day and although Peter was understanding and didn't hold it against him, Jay never forgave himself and has hated journalists ever since.'

'But I still don't get it,' Jo said. 'Why go to all this trouble? What have we ever done to you, Nikki?'

10

Roger Staverton looked up at the Great Neston Oak, where the body of Jacob swung in the early morning breeze. He clapped his hands angrily as a couple of crows flapped around, but they flew up into the large yew tree, waiting for him to leave.

There was a notice tacked to the tree, promising a painful death to anyone who attempted to cut the miscreant down. Roger snatched it off and tore it into tiny shreds.

'I swear to you, Jacob,' he said, his eyes swimming with tears, 'before this day is done I will put this right.'

Nikki looked warily at Seth, who sat, arms folded, glaring at her. 'That night Caroline came to see you, when she was in such a state, well we overheard what you were saying. We didn't mean to, of course, but the window was open and we couldn't help it.'

Seth snorted and was about to say something but Jo forestalled him. 'What did you overhear?' she asked.

'We heard Caroline tell Seth he had to do something about you,' she told Annabel. 'That you were his problem as much as hers. That he'd got away scot free until now but that it was about time he faced up to his responsibilities. Jay didn't get it, but I did. I knew straight away.' She faced Seth, her eyes defiant. 'You're her father, aren't you?'

'That's none of your business, Missy,' he snapped.

'You think not? Well, that's where you're wrong, Seth. Jay and me, we've got plans. Plans to get married. And that business of yours — ' She turned to Annabel, as if appealing to her. 'You see, he makes Jay work all hours of the day and night. For peanuts. Excuses it by saying he's ploughing the money back into the business and it'll all be his one day.'

'And so it will,' Seth said. 'But I still don't see what that's got to do with you, still less with the mess you and Jay have got yourself in.'

'Well, it's his inheritance,' Nikki muttered. 'If you suddenly find you've got yourself a daughter, then everything will be halved, won't it? And, well, I didn't think that was fair. Not fair on Jay, I mean, after all the work he's put into the business.'

'But I don't want anything from Seth, I can assure you,' Annabel said.

'But I wasn't to know that, was I?' Nikki said. 'But I really am sorry at the way things have turned out and that's the truth. I didn't know Jay was going to drug you or anything like that. I just meant him to keep you out of the way for a bit.'

'And how did you think he was going to do that?' Jo cut in, still simmering with anger towards Jay. 'Use his natural charm to ask Annabel out on a date?'

Nikki shrugged. 'He was just supposed to give her false directions, something like that. Send her off on some wild goose chase. But then he got this idea of leaving her in the attic room. I think he was going to frighten her into thinking the place was haunted or something. But then, when I said her sister was around, asking questions, well, he just panicked and that's when he got some of his mum's sleeping pills and put them in her coffee.'

She stopped as she heard Seth's sharp intake of breath and turned to Annabel. 'He thought they'd make you sleep for a couple of hours, no longer. He didn't mean you to be out for so long. It frightened him to death when he couldn't wake you.'

'I'll do more than frighten him to death when I catch up with him,' Seth promised angrily.

'But it didn't frighten him enough to call an ambulance, did it?' Jo retorted. 'Annabel could have had an allergic reaction. Anything could have happened. He is not going to get away with this.'

'He was on his way up to check on her again when you turned up, saying you knew where she was and that you were going to the police. That's when he lost it completely and locked you both in.'

'I don't know what to say,' Annabel said faintly.

'Anyway, I've told you the whole story now,' Nikki said. 'We didn't mean it to turn out like this, honest. And he was already on his way back to let you both out when you came down the stairs with Rob. Do you want scones with your tea? I could get you some if you like.'

'What?' Jo was completely thrown by the abrupt change of subject.

'No thanks,' Annabel said firmly. 'Now, if you'll excuse us, Seth and I still have things to talk about — and this time there'll be no listening at doors.'

She held the door open and waited until the girl had disappeared down the corridor then she turned back with a sigh, shaking her head.

'Look, I've not come here to plead Jay's case, nor Nikki's,' Seth said. 'And I have to say, what that girl came out with has shaken me a bit and all. I came because I felt it was about time someone told you the truth. And to apologise for all you've been through. And to apologise to you,' he turned to Jo, 'for being so rough on you in the pub.'

'Why did you do that?' Jo said indignantly, remembering how scared she'd been. 'And what was all that nonsense about Judy Garland?'

'I was trying to put you off. I could see the likeness when you showed me the photograph of Annabel and I knew there would be other folks around who'd make the same connection.'

'Judy Garland?' Annabel said faintly. 'Do I need to know this?'

Seth shook his head. 'Nikki told me you'd checked out and gone home. But then when your sister here comes into the pub saying you were missing, I didn't know what to think. I wanted her out of the way while I sorted things out. Then when I heard your car was in the rhine, I had a bad feeling Jay was involved. It's a favourite spot of his and — '

'My car is where?' Annabel asked.

'In a ditch,' Jo shivered at the memory. 'That's where Jay slipped off to in the pub, wasn't it? He heard me say I'd found Annabel's car by the church, so he drove it off and dumped it in a rhine.'

'The police know about it,' Seth said. 'They're charging him with car theft. What else they charge him with is up to you.'

'I don't know. I've got to think about it.' Annabel dragged her fingers through her hair. 'And about the fact that Caroline doesn't want to see me.'

Seth shook his head. 'I'm sorry. She says while Peter is unwell, she can't take the risk. She asked me to give you this.' He handed her an envelope, then stood up to go.

But he paused by the door, looked

back and cleared his throat. 'My wife and I, we never had a daughter. Just the one boy. I'd be proud to . . . well, any time you feel — Christ, I'm no good at this sort of thing.' He gave Annabel an anguished look. 'I'm sure you've had it up to here with the Carlson family and I don't blame you, but if you ever feel you want to know us better and give Jay the chance to make up a little for what he did to you — I promise you, he's not the monster you think he is. Just an idiot who's easily led. Well, the thing is, I'd be proud . . .'

'Thank you, Seth,' Annabel whispered. 'I'll — I don't really . . .'

'Well, you know where I am,' he said and left, closing the door softly behind him.

Annabel opened the envelope and read the brief note inside. Something fluttered to the floor and Jo picked it up and handed it to her. Annabel looked at it then tore it into pieces and dropped it in the waste basket.

'What was it?' Jo asked gently. 'Or

would you rather not tell me?'

'It's okay.' Annabel took a deep breath and Jo could see she was fighting back tears. 'She just said she's sorry, that Seth would explain everything. The other piece of paper was a cheque. To make up for all the birthdays she missed.'

'Annabel, I'm so sorry.'

'Don't be nice to me, Jo. You'll only set me off. For heaven's sake, this is your big chance to say I told you so. You said I should take things slowly, didn't you? But no, I had to rush in, feet first, as usual.' She crushed the note in her hand. 'First thing tomorrow,' she said as she dropped the crumpled letter in her handbag, 'I'm going home.'

'Good idea. But when are we going to the police?'

She shook her head. 'Provided my car is repaired, or replaced if need be, I'm not going to take things any further.'

'But you must. Jay committed a serious crime. He deserves all he gets.'

'I can't send my own brother to prison, can I?'

'And how do you feel about — about Seth?'

'Being my father?' Annabel shrugged with a brave attempt at nonchalance. 'I haven't a clue.'

Jo took her hand. As she did so, the phone rang. It was Rob.

'Jo? How are you both? Are you ready to go to the police yet?'

'We're much better, thanks. As for going to the police, we were just talking about that. Annabel's decided not to press charges.'

'She's not? Well, it's her decision.' Rob didn't sound convinced it was the right one, but he made no attempt to persuade her otherwise. 'Look, I know I've already asked once and you turned me down, but would you have dinner with me this evening? It would go some way to making up for the bump on the head I received earlier.'

'Dinner tonight? No, I can't.' Jo's cheeks burned. 'I'm sorry but Annabel needs me.'

The phone was snatched away.

'Annabel here, Rob. Jo would love to have dinner with you. I'd love her to have dinner with you, too. It would stop her clucking over me like a mother hen when really all I need is to veg out with some TV and an early night.'

She listened for a moment then hung up. 'He says he'll meet you in the hotel bar at eight o'clock, then take you to the best restaurant in Wells which — shame on him — he confesses isn't the hotel dining room.'

'How could you do that?' Jo looked at her sister in exasperation. 'How do you know you haven't set me up for dinner with a man I can't stand?'

'Because I saw the way he looked at you this afternoon. And if a man as attractive as him looked at me like that, I'd have dinner with him like a shot.'

'But I meant what I said. I don't want to leave you. Not tonight.'

'And I meant what I said. I promise you all I want is to have a bath, then curl up in bed with a glass of wine and the TV. I might even read some of

Caroline's book.'

She picked up the book, took it over to the chair by the window and began flicking through the pages.

'If you're sure,' Jo said.

'Hey, listen to this. The last page.'

'Oh, Annabel, you're not still reading the last page first, are you?'

'I know. I'm a hopeless case.' Annabel grinned, a full on, Annabel-type grin that made Jo's heart sing. 'But just listen to this, Jo.'

'It was midnight,' she read aloud. 'An owl flew past on silent wings as Roger Staverton approached the Great Neston Oak. He took out his knife and went up to the sorry remains of what once was Jacob. He cut the rope and, with infinite tenderness, wrapped Jacob in the sheet he'd brought with him. He carried him to the church where he'd already opened the Staverton family vault.'

'The family vault,' Jo said. 'It looks like the two were brothers after all.'

'Hang on,' Annabel said. 'There's more. He placed his dead friend alongside his father, said a prayer for his soul and begged forgiveness for what he was about to do.

'But his plea was directed only at the Almighty. He didn't seek forgiveness from his lady wife. He couldn't bring himself to call her by name. He could never forgive her for her part in Jacob's death. She'd used the fact that she was with child to justify what she'd done. She'd stood by and watched an innocent man hang.

'He hardened his heart against the unborn child. He wouldn't — he couldn't think of it. The only thought that filled his mind was that his dearest friend, his playmate from birth, the man who was more than a brother to him, had died a terrible death on his behalf.

'He left Jacob and went back to the Neston Oak, climbed on a box, placed the noose around his neck — and kicked the box away. His last thought in this world was what he'd say to Jacob in the next.

'This time,' he'd say, 'I took your place.'

There was silence in the room as Annabel finished reading. Jo was the first to break it. 'So Jacob really was Roger's brother?'

'Half-brother probably. You know how the local Lords of the Manor used to spread their favours about in those days.'

'It would explain the likeness though, wouldn't it?' Jo said. 'If they were related, I mean.'

'But it doesn't matter, does it?' Annabel said, her eyes bright, her cheeks flushed. 'Whether or not the two men were brothers by blood, it doesn't matter.'

She put the book down, walked across to Jo and hugged her. 'Sit down, Jo. Let's forget about Jacob Carlson for a moment. I've something to say, although for once in my life I'm not sure I've got the words. You know, for as long as I live I will never forget the sight of you handbagging poor Rob.' She giggled at the thought.

'I can't believe I did that,' Jo shook her head. 'I could have killed him.'

'That's my point. You, who has never had so much as a parking ticket and who always drives the right way around a supermarket car park, committed an act of considerable violence. What made you do it?'

'You're my sister and you needed help.'

'That's what I reckoned. It's what being family is all about, isn't it? And like with Roger and Jacob, it's not about biology. That's the least of it. Sure, I've got Seth's nose — curse him for that — and Caroline's whatever, but my character, the bit of me that really counts, I got from Mum and Dad, the same as you did. We're from the same emotional stock, you and I. That makes us more closely related than Jay Carlson and I could ever be. Do you see what I'm saying?'

Jo didn't trust her voice so she nodded and as she did so, a couple of tears slid down her cheeks.

'I'm okay,' Annabel went on. 'Better now than at any time since finding those wretched Adoption Papers.'

'I'm so glad. But — '

'And I'd really like you to go out with Rob tonight. Incidentally, he asked that you leave your shoulder bag behind.' She giggled again. 'Apparently, he's not too fond of it. So, to show you how much I want you to go, I'm prepared to let you borrow my Prada handbag. Just this once, mind.'

'You would? Then how can I refuse?' Jo said, while at the same time trying to think what she might have to go with such a special bag. Perhaps Annabel, whose taste in clothes was so much better than hers, would have something suitably stunning she could borrow.

After all, what else are sisters for?